FRONT TOWARD ENEMY

ROSS DAVIES

COPYRIGHT

Copy edits by Tristan Robson

Cover photo by Siobahn Alberts.

Cover design by Cassandra Duchesneau

ISBN-13

978-0986755736

REVISED FIRST EDITION

ACKNOWLEDGEMENTS

How do you truly summarize a decade of appreciation in paragraph? And if there were a way to do that, would it actually express the gratitude it should?

Probably not, because I haven't found a way to do that yet and I have written over a two hundred thousand words.

I think that this time instead of naming a bunch of people and thanking them, I am just going to say thank you and know that the people who deserve thanks know who they are. They already know this because they know what they have done for me. More so, they are satisfied that this novel is done and I'm still alive and doing what I love, which is writing. That this is all they have ever wanted for me, from me, and that is enough for them.

However, I will credit people by name and thank them for their artistic contribution, but beyond that, I will only thank one person by name personally, and that person is me. This book is for me, but I hope you enjoy reading it as much as I did writing it.

Sincerely, Ross A. S. Davies

PROLOGUE

A man in his mid-to-late twenties, soft olive skin, dark brown hair, with even darker brown eyes pulls himself down a beaten and empty road toward a nearby highway. Deep crimson blotches from blood splatter speckle his skin. His hair soaked by sweat pulled back off his forehead turning black from brown. His eyes are deep brown and pooled like dirty rainwater in red clay.

His onyx shirt is drawn open just above a gaping knife wound that spews further darkness into the shirt's already black fabric. He has both hands pressed firmly against the wound trying to keep the blood that runs freely from running at all.

He stops right before the highway and takes his left hand off the wound, puts it into his pocket, then takes it out, removing a cell phone; sliding it open he presses one key and with barely a second gone by someone answers,

"I'm here. Where are you?"

A short time later...

A car drives off the highway and pulls up in front of him. The driver, a middle-aged blonde woman, gets out and runs to his side, helping him to the passenger side door.

"Where is he?"

The man looks up at her from under his tired brow, one hand slides from her shoulder on to her neck and the other slides behind her, settling on the small of her back. She immediately goes stiff, taken back by his unwarranted advance, fearing his touch.

"He is still in the diner. Get me out of here..."

He looks into her eyes, smirking slightly, and then he forcefully kisses her, and for a moment, she hesitates, but when she tastes him, she gives in completely and kisses back. She pulls him closer now, forcing him in, savagely. He consumes her, as though possessed by him. Now she pushes her body into his, trying to tear free clothes, and then, suddenly and forcefully, he pushes her away.

"Now."

Hypnotized, she jumps to his command, throwing the door open for him; she helps him in without question.

He leans his head back, trying to seek comfort that he knows won't come. He has lost too much blood, and the luxury of time is something he does not know. He looks at her; his eyes command her without words because she lingers at his door. He nods to her to move, and she does. She closes the door and runs around the car, clipping quickly in her heels, magically retaining her balance. She climbs into the car, slamming her door. She throws the car into the drive and gases it, accelerating immediately and in her immediacy the car tails out a trail of dirt and dust.

"Where do you want to go?" She says, reaching across and stroking his dark locks, pinching them between her fingers.

"The nearest hotel or motel." He swats her hand away, and points ahead to the road.

"Did he do that to you?"

"Yes. Yes, he did. Alex, stop looking at me and pay attention to the road."

"I can't help it. I'm worried."

"No, Alex, you feel compelled to worry, but you really aren't. Do you have a cigarette?"

"Glove box…and don't say that." She says, injured, staring at him with doe eyes filled to the lids with liquid. Her gaze is fixed to him as he digs through the glove box for the cigarettes, and she salivates when he shoves one between his swollen lips. His eyes snap over as he struggles to light it, and he stops trying when he sees her.

"Alex, pay attention to the fucking road." He grabs her chin and forcefully turns her gaze to the road. She doesn't detest or mind his force; she relishes his attention.

"Sorry..."

She pulls into a motel, as he finishes his cigarette. She runs to the office as he sits up smoking another one, clinging to consciousness. She helps him out of the car after returning from the office and leads him into a room. She closes the door as he walks through it and slowly, painfully, removes his black jacket and then his blood-soaked black shirt. He stands in front of the bed with both hands on his wound, rocking back and forth before taking incremental inhales and drawn-out exhales of air, searching for coherence.

"What can I do?"

"Did you bring me what I asked you to?" Without looking back at her, he questions, his voice barely breaks through his breathing.

"Yeah, it's in the car."

"Go. Get. He says through closed crimson clenched teeth, barely containing the fury for her lack of sense and if he could, he would unleash it on her but the life it would take to scorn her; he knows he neither has nor could spare. Every little ounce, or rather shred, he has left goes to retaining focus.

She does what he commands, without question, still completely enchanted. As she leaves the room he stumbles to the bathroom. He opens the shower door and steps in, kicking his pants on the washroom floor. He closes the door behind him and turns on the water. As the cold stream becomes warm, he falls, sliding down with his back against the shower wall. He lets the blood run from his stomach as he looks at the wound. Clean stab: blade went in clean, came out clean. He wonders how much blood he has lost, and reminds himself if it is more than forty percent; he is dead. He hears her come in and lock the door and then make her way into the washroom.

"I have what you asked for."

He turns off the water and opens the shower door. He sits naked, with his hands out. She hands him a medical bag. He opens it and removes anti-bacterial disinfectant. With his other hand he takes the bottle of whisky she is holding and opens it with his thumb and index, unscrewing the cap. He takes a large swig and then sprays the disinfectant on the wound. He takes the saline solution out of the bag and sprays that over the wound. He grabs a needle and suture thread from the bag and takes a deep inhale and then he looks up to Alex. She stands there in the doorway to the shower watching: unflinching, completely motionless, and just gazes down at him.

"Alex, suture me—but first—give me your phone."

She kicks off her shoes and goes to her knees pulling her phone from her pocket, she hands it to him and takes the suture and thread and crawls between his legs. He opens the phone and dials a number. As the phone rings on and on, she steadies her hand and awaits his go ahead.

The call goes to voicemail, and he speaks,

"Valentyne, I wish you could've been a tad more professional in resigning your position..."

He nods and she buries the needle into the skin through the other side pulling the thread across and his voice doesn't change.

"...However, I understand your need to pursue other career options, and we will surely miss you."

He hangs up the phone and tosses it above Alex's back, it clatters in the sink, and she continues suturing his wound, unconcerned for her possessions. He reaches into her dress jacket and removes a pack of cigarettes and a small lighter. She continues to suture. He takes a cigarette out and lights it, taking a deep inhale, he lets his head fall back against the wall. She cuts the thread at the knot and sits up staring at him.

He blows a ring of smoke at her face and then he smiles,

"Thank you."

Her eyes gloss and she smirks, her cheeks barely form into dimples as she removes her fogged glasses. She runs one hand up his right ankle, following the tail of a tattoo, a jet-black snake tail spirals up his leg, running up and around his calf and over his groin and up into the head of a cobra stopping just under his belly button.

"No Alex, not now. Go lay down on the bed, I'll be there soon."

She smiles and stands, turning, she goes back into the bedroom. He sits up, removing bandages from the bag, placing them over the sutured wound. He grabs a roll of adhesive tape, which he bites four pieces from and dresses his wound, covering the bandages to hold over the wound. The white quickly turns red. He takes a long inhale and then looks at his whisky. He takes a large swig, swallows a mouthful, and then blows out a plume of smoke before closing his eyes.

Twenty-four hours later he sits lurched over himself at the foot of the bed, smoking a cigarette clutching his stomach, watching the news.

"The only suspect in what we can call a midnight rampage escaped from a police escort and is now at large in the area. If you have any details please contact the authorities immediately, do not try and apprehend the suspect yourself, he is considered extremely dangerous."

They flash a sketch of their suspect and release his "suspected" identity.

"Johnny Valentyne, once thought to be deceased is now at large."

He shuts off the television and turns to look back at the lifeless Alex, who is tangled up in the sheets with no visible trauma, but she isn't breathing. Her eyes are faded and glossy. Bile encrusts the corners of her lips. Her skin is pale and clammy. She is dead. He sighs and grabs his cigarettes and jacket. He puts his feet back into his shoes and he walks out the door.

He drives down the highway, watching the signs pass, pointing him to the hospital and he follows.

He drives right up to the emergency entrance at the hospital and gets out, stumbling through the automatic doors. He falls down on the ground as doctors and nurses rush over to help him.

When they get him on a stretcher, they try and keep him conscious by asking him questions. They ask him obvious questions, like "Do you know where you are?" he smiles in response.

They wheel him down the hall and ask him more obvious questions, like "What is your name?" he smiles and speaks up, "Johnny." They ask him another question, "Johnny what?" He doesn't pause. "Johnny Valentyne." One doctor runs back to the check in station at the emergency entrance and calls somebody.

In a week from today, another Johnny Valentyne will walk through those automatic doors covered in blood. I know this because I'm Johnny Valentyne. I'll be here in a week.

THERE ARE NO SUCH THINGS AS HAPPY ENDINGS

Freedom is and will always be just a concept. I get back to a life I unintentionally left behind and I let it unintentionally slip away. It is nearly impossible to imagine that things hadn't changed and when I realize they had, well, I'm not really a fan of change.

How can I be? You have this idea in your head about how love is supposed to be stronger than any other force. That love is all you need, just like the Beatles song. That idea is something that makes you smile, feel whole, or in my case, kill your way out of a bad situation. The idea is beautiful, but realistically, it is just an idea. Just like a wound, it'll heal, but it leaves something. A scar and now, I have more than I want to count.

I stand in front of a large mirror opening and closing my jaw. I'm in a small very bright bathroom with canary yellow walls. In front of the mirror is a bright and sparkling porcelain sink with brass faucet and matching brass valves for hot and cold. The toilet is porcelain and very clean, sparkling ivory. The tub is deep and again made from porcelain; it to is gorgeous and shining, and it stands on four iron legs. I look back in the mirror. I lean closer.

My five o'clock shadow is dark and coarse; it started at five o'clock, seventy-two hours ago. I pull my hand through my dark brown hair and as I do, I expose my ear. I look at my mangled ear and I take a step back, looking at each of my new wounds. The bandages are white and the adhesive tape holding them there pulls back on each corner as they lose their stick. I can feel the skin around the sutures pulling tight with every miniature move. Every time I look upon these wounds, I am comforted by the certainty Sketch is dead.

Better yet, I'm not, and I'm not on the run.

Twenty-four hours after my dramatic and highly unexpected rescue, the police stop looking for me. I know, you're thinking what I'm thinking. Why the hell would they stop?

It turns out I showed up at a hospital with a very nasty stomach wound. According to the news, the suspect, me, shows up at a hospital with a wound that he tried to treat himself. Not even five hours after the police began looking for me because I had escaped from an armed escort.

Now, I know, that they will soon know, if not, already know, that the guy they have in custody isn't me. Now, only a medical record could prove that. I mean, he fits my description; actually, the guy is almost identical to me except for these bullet wounds that were treated in the trauma center at that hospital.

I guess it is hard to confirm someone's identity that has been dead for six or more years. Then again, the only real connection Johnny Valentyne has is Jessica Mackenzie and the only proof of their relationship was an insurance claim that probably won't see the light of day. Then again, this is all speculation. They don't know anything about Manny or Max; we have no affiliation on paper, and we didn't go to school together. Even when the truck used to assault the escort was stolen from Max's work. They can't put us together. So, Manny doesn't need an alibi. Max has one but doesn't need one. The only one that might need one is Jess, and she has several.

I know I am far from comfortable, but at least I have one less thing to worry about. Even though it isn't really one less thing, because the person they have in custody is in fact a threat to me.

"Johnny."

I spin around and there is Jess standing in the doorway. She just stares at me.

"Yeah?"

She continues to stare, expressionless.

"Jess?"

"Yeah, sorry."

She shakes her head and shrugs.

I look back in the mirror.

"Every-time I see you it is like seeing a ghost."

I look at her through the reflection in the mirror.

"You know I'm very much alive."

"You're different."

I scratch my face.

"Yeah, I can't help that, but at least I'm alive. It could be worse..."

"You were dead Johnny. I let you go."

I turn around. My eyebrows fall. My forehead scrunches and I sigh.

"...but I'm not. I cannot imagine what it felt like, to lose me, to let me go, but you brought me back. I came back for you."

"No, Johnny, you came back for you. I moved on. I know this isn't fair, but things have changed, my feelings have changed."

"How? Doesn't this make you feel something."

I grab her hand and put it on my chest. I kiss her and she kisses back but only momentarily before pushing me back.

"Of course, it feels like something, but it tastes like yesterday. Johnny, I don't feel the same way anymore."

"Then why didn't you just let me go to jail."

"Because you deserve to be happy, to live, it isn't fair what happened to you. I thought I could be with you, have you back, to have it like it was but it won't be. You're different. Johnny, I just want you to be happy. But I can't make you happy."

"You do make me happy. Being back with you makes me happy. I came back because of you. I felt how much I missed you even when I didn't know you existed. Your memory gave me mine back."

"You aren't happy. You never could lie to me so don't try to start now. It is behind your eyes. You're miserable."

"I'm not miserable. Jess, I love you, please don't do this. You told me we'd work things out, don't give up, we need time."

"I've had a lot of time Johnny, so much time away from you, and things have changed. My feelings have changed. I wish they hadn't, but they have. I love you but in a different way. I'm so sorry Johnny."

"You feel something, or you wouldn't be here. You wouldn't have helped me. You wouldn't have fucked me."

"Of course I would. I told you; I love you in a different way. Of course, I'm still attracted to you, but I don't love you in the same way."

"Are you even listening to what you're saying?"

"Please, don't make this any harder than this is Johnny."

"It isn't hard. Well, it isn't right now."

I smile, looking down at myself.

She holds back the tears and laughs.

"Be serious. Please."

"I don't want to be. You want me Jess, you always do, don't do this to yourself, to me, or us. You're confused and you have the right to be."

"She isn't confused...Are you ok Jess?"

Steven walks up from behind Jess.

"Hey, buddy, this isn't your business."

"Yes, it is."

Jess shakes her head.

"What kind of guy is ok with his "girlfriend" fucking somebody else? Take a hint Steven, things are complicated enough, she obviously doesn't know what she wants but let me tell you, it ain't you."

Jess pushes me back.

"Johnny. Enough. Steven please, I need to talk to Johnny."

"Didn't you hear what she was telling you Johnny? It sounds to me like she isn't confused, sounds like she is trying to move on."

"Steven!"

Steven nods at Jess and walks away.

"He knows I've killed people, right?"

Jess' face crumples into a frown, she looks away briefly and returns with an expression that makes me miserable.

"Johnny. Please. Steven is part of my life now. You're right, I am confused, but Steven makes me happy..."

"You fuck me and help me evade prison because you care about Steven, how idiotic I have been, that is so obvious now."

She slaps me on the face and all I do is smile.

"Johnny, please, I need to do this. If you love me, you'd want me to be happy."

"I do and this guy won't. If he did, you wouldn't have done what you did for me or you wouldn't have fucked me right before you guys went to lunch and not tell him. Both are pretty fucking substantial arguments to how I know you aren't going to be happy with this guy, but hell, maybe I should ask him what he thinks."

"Johnny. Please."

"Jess, you aren't making any sense."

"Johnny, please, it is what I want. I'm sorry."

Tears well in my eyes but stay as I draw in a long deep would-be endless inhale.

"Fine."

I walk past Jess and walk into her bedroom. I grab my grey boxer-brief underwear, pulling them up. I grab my jeans, putting them on. I grab a pair of black socks. I grab a black t-shirt, yanking it over my head, and threading my arms through each sleeve as quick as I can. I go to the night side table of my makeshift bed, and collect them, and everything I own: one black wallet, no identification cards but a couple of small bills; a new lighter and a pack of cigarettes; and finally, keys to a burned down house and a destroyed car.

I pocket everything but my smokes.

I open them; removing a cigarette, I toss it in my mouth. I turn back to the doorway, which Jess now occupies.

"Johnny. I'm so sorry."

"I know. So am I."

I slide past her, her watery eyes, and sympathy-ridden jaw, and down the hallway and downstairs to the first floor. Steven stands by the living room popping two pills from an antihistamine package. I look at him and if I didn't have the ability to restrain myself right now, I'd have him pinned to the ground with my hands on his throat choking the life from his smug face. His expression changes and something overtakes it slightly, surprising me.

"Johnny, listen, I know this is all fucked up but if it means anything, I'm sorry."

I walk past him and throw my untied black steel-toed work boots on.

"I know this isn't your fault but understand me, if any harm comes to her, I'll kill you."

He looks to the ground ashamed. I open the door and hit the porch. I stop and light my cigarette. I look around and then walk. I hit the sidewalk, and keep on walking down, leaving the house behind me with no idea where to go, I walk on, aimless.

I just want to get as far away from here as I can, and I fight the feeling that tries to sink in. I want to ignore what just happened, she is just confused, scattered. She'll come around. It is too early for this shit and with that, I want coffee. I grab a bus and head for the closest place to grab coffee.

I stand in a line behind four others. Every couple seconds, I look back at the large, windowed doors that are only several feet away, warily. Two big panes of glass held into red steel frames. Beyond those doors a small foyer where you have the option of wiping your feet. Beyond the foyer, two more large, windowed doors held together by more red steel frames. Beyond those doors the outside. I'm left wondering about several things while this five-person line has not gotten any shorter. One of those several thoughts being:

Are these doors shatterproof?

I look back to the line as it loses a person as they head to the bar waiting for their very pretty beverage with so many names. I want coffee.

Now I am within earshot of the next customer who orders another pretty drink with even more names.

All I want is coffee. This takes me to my next thought, the next in line, and the next to go to the bar and wait for those really pretty drinks with way too many names. This brings me to my last thought. Why don't they have a place to order and pay for coffee and have cash at the bar so those patrons can pay for those extremely pretty drinks with too many names. That way you split up the time because if it worked that way, I wouldn't be standing in line, I'd be sitting outside, enjoying the morning sun, looking over my shoulder.

I realize that the last thought could be interpreted as unsettling and so will my justification. Yes, I'm paranoid, but I'm also very observant. I can appreciate what's around me and it's not always someone trying to kill me, kidnap me, or arrest me...

"How can I help you?"

I turn my attention to my barista. A petite blonde with a creamy white skin, glowing red lips, grey-blue eyes, and a blinding white smile that lifts exposing perfect pink gums. I instinctively close my mouth, pursing my lips, pondering, hiding my cracked yellow smile. "Large coffee please."

My eyebrows lift as she stares at me, holding an empty cup.

One eyebrow climbs above the other expressing my mild confusion. Waiting for her to ask me what she wants to ask me.

She smiles, and then speaks, asking me a question: "Room for milk or room for cream?"

"Room for milk, please, I don't like cream."

I smile, at first innocently, but as she turns so does my smile, wickedly. I chuckle as I tap my knuckles on the laminated wooden counter.

When she returns, her face has changed, and her body language as well, she carries no definable expression. She robotically slides my coffee over to me as I pass her exact change, without her asking, I know the price, two dollars and ten cents. Her eyes stay on me as I go to walk away. I stop and turn as I catch her stare, kept on me, unflinching.

It quickly shifts as she tries to pretend, she wasn't staring and when she acknowledges my smile, she smiles, mimicking me. She looks better from far away, but still not right, different from the girl she was when I first spoke to her.

As I start to turn and so does, she, something happens in her expression. It quickly changes as her eyes roll back briefly and then return as she shakes her head to fight something, maybe exhaustion, maybe something else, maybe something like recognition.

"You, okay?" I pipe up.

She looks over at me and throws a quick smile.

"Yeah. I'm fine. It's just a headache. I've had it all morning, but I took some Advil and it's going away." She says, smiling through glassy eyes.

"Thanks."

"Have a good day." I say, smiling.

"Thanks, you too."

As she turns to leave, I watch her and her gorgeous stride. I then notice a small basket next to the counter. In the basket: half-liter bottles of water. Each bottle is four dollars and ninety-nine cents before taxes. The sign above the basket says proceeds will help bring fresh water to third world countries.

Why not just send the water there?

I walk over to a small station where you add whatever you want to your coffee. This station is conveniently placed near the front doors, slightly to the right of them. There I can make my coffee just the way I like it. Enough milk so it's red and two sugar packets later, it's ready, and I take a sip of it. I close my eyes and take a deep breath. I hold my breath for a moment, let it out, and I open my eyes as I drink more hot coffee.

I walk through one set of double doors. Out through the foyer and then out through the second set of double doors into the bright morning light.

I'm blinded momentarily but not to the point where I don't see the cop walking toward me. I hold the door open with my foot; I turn my head and look over for a vacant table and smile, as if they're all vacant. He stops, looks at me, pauses for a moment, which appears to be some sort of examination.

Or is it recognition?

He winces, removes a bottle of Tylenol and pops two, and nods, thanking me, as he walks by,

"Thanks." Confirming his appreciation vocally.

"No problem."

I walk over and sit down at the very first vacant table. I take several swigs of coffee, and I sit back enjoying the blinding and warm glow from the fiery orb that lights the morning.

Like popping a balloon, like fireworks going off, or even better, yeah much closer, a gun goes off. The chair goes over first, followed by a table, and I'm over it. I'm sprinting at the doors.

They aren't shatter proof.

I'm running full board into the coffee shop in a rain of glass, sliding through the second set of doors I've just thrown open, and I witness the cop, unloading a gun into absolute strangers. Innocent fucking bystanders, people just there to get a coffee or some strange, caffeinated beverage with eight different names.

He's gunned down a couple, one of the baristas, and he's now aiming that standard issue 9mm Glock at a woman protecting her child. That slide becomes a jolt forward, bull rushing him into the glass display that holds overpriced cookies, sandwiches, drinks, and donuts beautifully displayed, enticing and in wait of purchase.

The glass shatters instantaneously as I put him through it. I throw my elbow into his arm and the Glock now points at the ceiling as a round tears from the barrel and destroys a light. My other hand swings under his arms catching his Adams apple roughly. While my other arm goes back with my hand wrapping around the barrel, I slide my finger over the clip disengage, and the clip drops out. I turn his wrist in the opposite direction punching his forearm with an open palm before I constrict my grip on it.

With my hand firmly on the gun, I attempt to remove it from his rigor mortis grip. His fingers constrictively hold the pistol like it is a part of his hand. The gun I can't retrieve and it's got one live round ready to tear from the barrel.

He now moves both his hands, dragging my arms down, dragging the gun back down. I try to look him in the eye as we fall, sliding from the broken display before smashing down on the granite tiling below us. When we hit the tiles, we lock eyes briefly, his glazed eyes and beyond their glassy surface, nothing. I have seen this look enough to know it and know it well. As though it is a place, I have frequented a thousand times, like a person I have known my entire life, as though a lover I never stopped loving.

That all too familiar expression. That look comes with, no emotion, no tears, no anger, absolutely nothing. No micro expression, no realization, and no sickness. It is like nothing is there, just a shell, shed like a skin for somebody else to use or wear.

It isn't a struggle as he overpowers me, dragging the gun. I throw one knee into his chest while yanking at his hands, trying to reposition their location. I begin to feel helpless as each hit and each pull yields the same result, he is pointing this gun where he wants to, and at the moment I can't stop him.

When that last bullet leaves the chamber, it tears from under his chin, through his mouth and cuts out of his brain lodging somewhere in dry wall.

I release him and rise, shaken and confused.

People slowly come back into the coffee shop when they realize it is safe. I feel their eyes. I look around to see cell phones pointed at me and some call for help.

Those pointed at me are recording, recording this whole scene, instead of—I don't know—helping me, they're recording.

I spin in place; I see that blonde barista, staring at me. Something is wrong. She is expressionless like my dead cop friend was and I have seen this face too many times. She holds something in her hand.

"Hey, are you ok?"

I speak in a soft voice, monotone.

People around me gasp, or cry, or ask me if I'm ok, or celebrate my heroics but I focus on this girl who wears that face.

The girl is wielding something, and I don't like not knowing what she hides behind her back. I try to appear calm even though I'm covered in the fresh gore of the cop. I take a step forward and she takes two back. She stares on, as though she is looking past me without acknowledging me, as though I'm not there. When I take another step forward, her back hits the sink behind her and as I climb over, she steps forward unveiling the hidden object.

Just my luck, she has a knife, a big knife.

She swipes at me, and I fall backward. She leaps over the counter, and I hear the pedestrian crowd gasp and cry out warning me of what I already know. I fall next to the dead cop, and she falls on top of me stabbing downward. I move out of the way of the blade even though she now straddles me and when that second stab comes down, I grab her wrists. I throw us over, toppling us on our sides and I smash her hands on the brown-red tiles. The knife scatters out of her grasp and slides across the floor. She lunges at it, but I catch her by the waist and her head smashes face first into the tile knocking her cold.

"What the fuck is going on?"

A man speaks up.

"Has everyone lost their minds?"

A woman cries.

I stand up.

"Did someone call the cops?"

I say, looking around. Fear paints the face of eight people. Four people stand watching. The other four try desperately to stabilize the wounded couple and wounded barista.

"Yeah, they are on their way."

The talkative amateur cameraman speaks up from behind his cell phone. The cell phone points at me.

"Buddy, you were amazing..."

He falls hard as I lay a fist into his jaw and his phone spins off under a table. I walk outside; people shout at me, some beg for me to stay, some give permission for me to leave, and the cameraman moans questioningly.

I leave my coffee, lonely on the table outside; I glance at it as I walk by.

I walk down the sidewalk of the strip-mall the coffee shop it's built into. I search for the signs of sirens, lights, police or ambulance but I don't see any.

I'm stopped in my tracks as a car flies over the curb right in front of me, so close I feel it fly by, and slams into the front window of a shoe store, decimating the front foyer and all glass of the main entrance and continuing into the busy store.

I hear screaming; I hear horns, and more accidents nearby. Cars crash, people fighting, people screaming for help and I stand motionlessly spinning around watching the chaos.

Vibration wakes me from my trance as I remove my phone; I have two missed calls, and one voicemail.

What the fuck is going on...

I walk on vigilantly trying to hear what the voicemail says while trying to avoid people and any other dangers.

Am I dreaming?

Or having a nightmare?

Message —

"Johnny…pick up please. Listen, something is wrong. Steven is acting strange…someone left a package on the porch for you…he opened it…and now…"

I hear banging. I hear her scream.

"…Please come back."

I hear her shouting.

"Steven! Stop!"

I hear more banging.

"Steven please, you're scaring me!"

Then she screams, dropping the phone.

I hear something smash, something loud, like a door breaking.

"Steven what're you doing?"

Then a gunshot and I flinch. Another has my heart in my stomach. Followed by another and another and then I hear her gasping, and I hear something crunch.

End of message —

My phone is back in my pocket, and I am running. It is a twenty-minute walk from Jess' house to this strip-mall; I will make it in five.

I SHOULD'VE STAYED "HOME" TODAY

The fun thing about pain—physical pain—is once you've hurt yourself enough, had someone hurt you enough, taken enough damage, you lose sensitivity. Pain stops being painful, well, physical pain at least. You get used to the sting of it. You become familiar with the feeling. The same concept, however, does not apply to emotional pain.

Like when the person you love, the person you fought to stay alive for, fought to come home for; tells you that she doesn't love you, like you love her.

That fucking kills.

Nothing can prepare you for watching that person you love die and there isn't a goddamn fucking thing you can do.

That is the most painful moment. Witnessing that and nothing—and I mean nothing—can or will ever compare...

When I come through that front door all I could hear is clicking.

When I get upstairs, I realize that clicking is Steven pulling the trigger over and over on an empty gun, standing in front of Jess, who is motionless, sprawled, bleeding out, and turning the beige of her carpet brown.

Steven is out cold in seconds. Now in desperation to get her back to consciousness and stop the bleeding, I'm screaming and watching the blood seep out from every hole an entire clip of a Glock can put into somebody. Ten rounds: ten holes.

I free a blanket from the bed pushing it down hard on her chest with one hand and dialing the ambulance with another. The phone just rings and rings as I push down harder with my other hand and watch as the blanket sucks up the blood, I hang up and redial.

I move her slightly and pull the blanket under and around her tight making a tourniquet on her entire torso, pulling tight. All while the phone just rings and rings. Finally, it connects but I don't get a dispatcher, I get an automated message.

Message—

"Emergency services are unavailable at this time, if you have an injury, seek medical attention at your nearest health provider or emergency room."

End of message—

"What the fuck..."

I say aloud as I close my phone and when I do, she opens her eyes with a weak inhale and then she speaks.

"Johnny...you came back?"

"Of course I did baby, stay with me, ok?"

"Why did Steven...why did Steven...why did he shoot me?"

"I don't know baby. I have to move you, ok?"

"No, it hurts...just stay with me..."

"No, jellybean...just stay with me. I'm going to bring you to the hospital...you'll be fine...baby, I survived, you have to for me, okay?"

She nods so slowly staring up at me; she's gone white as the white of the sheet she is wrapped in, or at least as white as the sheet was.

I hoist her slowly into my arms and rise. I walk down the stairs and down the hall grabbing Stevens' car keys.

I walk out through the already open front door and open Steven's car electronically. I slide into the driver's seat with her cradled onto my lap.

I start the car and peel out almost clipping another car as it slams into a parked one. I push the car to its absolute.

Her head limply hangs on my shoulder, and I kiss her forehead.

"Johnny. I'm sorry."

"Baby...don't. It is going to be fine. We will be laughing about this soon."

"J..ohn...ny it isn't fun...ny"

"Jellybean stay with me. Sing me a song, okay? I want you to sing that song from camp for me. Sing baby."

"There...was a great big...moose..."

I shake her.

"...he liked to drink..."

"What did he like to drink baby?"

I shake her and she opens her eyes.

"He liked to drink a lot of juice, banana."

She smiles and starts to close her eyes, and I push the accelerator further, cornering hard, I release it but only for a moment and then smash it down to the ground.

I pass by fires, car accidents, and screaming pedestrians. Chaos and struggle at every few feet.

I maneuver through traffic, human and vehicle alike. I try to divide my focus between all of the commotion and her.

I shake her,

"Baby, the great big moose, who liked to drink a lot of juice, what did he sing? Baby!"

She opens her eyes and slowly shakes her head as the color in her face is all but gone.

"Singin' way-o way-o..."

"Way-o way-o way-o way-o."

She doesn't respond, so I kiss her head hard, as I'm not far from the hospital now.

"Baby!"

She doesn't answer.

"Baby! Wake up!"

She doesn't answer.

"Jellybean!"

I scream.

She opens those beautiful eyes and smiles.

"Baby...shush...I'm tired."

The blanket is completely soaked in her blood as, are my clothes. With each word, she wheezes, and it takes her longer to finish each sentence.

"We're almost there just hang on."

I pull into the hospital entrance speeding past parked cars and car wrecks, there are people everywhere, some run, some walk, some are injured, and others are motionless, and I assume some of them are dead.

There are people lying in the grass and some on the pavement. I pull into the emergency section ignoring the 'no parking' zones, sliding and braking right in front of the automated doors of the emergency entrance.

I open the door and gently carry her in, trying to get her to speak, to give me a sign of life. She is still, loosely and limply cradled in my arms, and I have carried her in this state far too often.

I walk through the doors into the chaos of the foyer, packing in with two-dozen strangers near the check in.

I stop in shock as too much is going on and I'm sick and scared and then suddenly I scream,

"Somebody help her!"

I scream so loud that I gain the attention of the panic and bustling people, the nurses, and the doctors. I stand in the open automated doors; holding her, soaked in scarlet.

Two doctors cut through the crowd with a gurney, shouting for people to move. I lay her down, they rush her down a hallway, and I follow not letting go of her hand.

"Sir, what happened?"

"She was shot; ten times, by a Glock 9mm. I found her ten minutes ago. I tried to stop the bleeding but there are so many..."

"Get me a crash cart. We need to get her into surgery now!"

He screams at a male nurse that runs up behind me.

"What is her name?"

"Jess Mackenzie."

"And yours?"

"Johnny Valentyne."

Jess, the gurney, one doctor and I keep going while the other one stops and stares at me, more stirred than he was a second ago. I look at him and he shakes it off and catches up.

"Please, save her."

"We will do our best. Now wait..."

"No, I want to stay with her."

"...Wait here, you can't come with us. I promise I will do everything I can, but look around; things are out of hand as is. Please, wait here."

He pushes me back and I lose grip of her hand. I watch her eyes close, and that peaceful smile slowly seeps from her expression and in horror, I watch as they disappear behind solid double doors.

I don't move. I stand there, watching the doors, frozen. I want to wake up, but I know this isn't a dream, I just wish it was.

From behind me, through the crying and the moaning I hear gasping as people in unison watch something in awe.

This breaks me from my trance as the television in the foyer broadcasts answers and I make my way back down the hallway to find out what everyone is gasping at,

"We are advising people to stay inside. If you are not seriously injured, please avoid going outside. If you see signs of this illness in your loved ones, keep them away from anything that can be used as a weapon.

Restrain them and wait for the authorities. We don't know the cause but if you see anyone and they appear as if in a trance, if they don't respond, they have contracted it and are extremely dangerous. We don't know the cause, but we are doing everything to resolve this and find the source..."

"What about emergency response?"

A reporter questions the speaker.

"...At this time, they are unable to respond to any urgency as they are handling what they have the manpower for...

"Is this localized or nation-wide?"

Another reporter barks a question.

"...At the moment it is localized, and we have requested assistance of the military...

"Do you expect this to spread?"

"...We don't know at this time. As soon as we have some sort of answer, any idea, we will respond in time.

We are just asking for patience and cooperation, as we are all victims of whatever this is. Please, no more questions, as soon as we know something, you will know."

The speaker leaves the podium, and it cuts back to a speechless anchorwoman.

"We urge residents to be patient, and we will return shortly."

The picture cuts into the coloured bar code that hums away with an endless beep as the transmission gets severed.

I whisper the word fuck.

"You alright?"

I turn and look at the person standing beside me, staring at me, wide-eyed with his jaw hanging open. This guy is around my age. Shorter than me by four to five inches with a dusty brown well maintained beard, sporting a flat cap on his head, hiding a dyed and rugged fashion mullet.

"Dude, are you alright?"

He asks again.

I blink several times before looking at myself.

I'm covered in her blood; drenched in it. It snakes up my hands around my wrists and coats my forearms. My jeans are dyed crimson from my crotch down to my knees and my shirt at stomach level is still soaking, dripping with it.

"Maybe you should sit down bro."

He points to a seat, extending his hand.

"Are you hurt?"

He asks as I follow him to the chairs.

As I sit down, I look over at him.

"No...it's not...it's not my blood."

"We don't have to talk about it man. I'm Zachary, Zachary Hart."

Over his voice and through the chaos of the emergency rooms I hear running. Hard boots smack roughly on linoleum.

I turn and look at him as he extends his hand about to introduce myself when...

"I'm Johnny..."

"Johnny Valentyne, don't move, just stay where you are. Slowly lift your hands and place them behind your head...do it now!"

A voice calls out from the corridor to the left of where I'm sitting. I don't look even when the request is backed up by the sound of cocking guns. Finally, when I feel like it, I turn my gaze and look at two police officers pointing guns at me.

Zachary doesn't move, doesn't flinch, and doesn't seem bothered that police are pointing guns at me.

"Whoa, guys, look around. This guy..."

He points at me.

"...whatever he did, is the least of your problems..."

He looks at me to validate his objections.

"...you didn't kill anyone right? That isn't where the blood came from?"

I shake my head no.

"...See, he is the least of your..."

"Sir, step away from him please."

"No. I mean, man, come on, look around, shouldn't you be helping people? This guy isn't hurting anyone."

"Sir. Step away from him, now!"

One cop points his gun at Zachary while the other one, and his gun, stay fixed on me.

Zachary goes to speak but I cut him off.

"Thanks man…"

I look at Zachary.

"…It was nice meeting you, I appreciate what you're trying to do, but don't involve yourself. Guys, focus, cuff me."

Zachary shakes his head, stands up, and walks past the first of the encroaching cops.

As the closer cop holsters his gun and goes for his cuffs, I move. I push from the chair so quickly it slides backward smashing into the row of chairs behind it. I kick hard into his right knee and throw a fist into his throat. While he recovers, I grab his Glock, turning it on him quickly, placing it against his temple, spinning him to face his partner while I dig the barrel deeper into his skin.

I do this all within the time the other cop takes— who still has his gun out—is just now past Zachary, now looking at his partner, my hostage.

"Put it down or so help me, you…"

I push harder against the cop's temple with the barrel of the Glock.

"…and him will be just two more causalities to this chaos. And please. Do not fucking test me."

Zachary stands there in the corridor, shocked, and frozen,

"Holy shit bro."

The cop doesn't move his gun.

"Don't do this."

He orders me.

"Put your fucking gun down."

I order back.

I tighten my grip with my forearm around his partner's throat pushing the barrel harder.

"Cuff yourself..."

I tighten my grip, my focus split between my hostage and his gun-wielding partner.

"...Put your fucking gun down, this is the last time I'm going to ask."

His partner lowers the pistol and drops it.

"You guys can arrest me when I know she is ok."

"You're making a mistake..."

The cop says as he raises his hands as his partner cuffs himself.

"Don't. Don't fucking reason with me, guilt me, try to tell me what I'm doing, because, trust me buddy, you have no idea. Now, your turn, cuff yourself."

I look past the cops at Zachary who turns and looks down the hallway and something has his attention and like nothing is going on he walks away.

When the other cop cuffs himself I throw his partner into the chairs and walk over with my gun pointed at the cop who has freshly cuffed himself.

"Back up."

He walks backward and I walk over and retrieve his gun.

"Sit down."

He walks over and sits down near his partner.

"Don't move. If I even, see you guys come after me. I'll shoot you."

"Don't do this Johnny. You're making things worse for you."

"Shut the fuck up. If you care about anything other than your job, you'll un-cuff yourself when I leave and you'll go to it if you're smart because the longer you waste your time on me when you get back to whatever you love, it won't not be there."

I turn and walk down the corridor where they took Jess, a Glock in each hand, everyone nearby scatters or hides with the exception of Zachary who stands with a red-haired girl at the end of the corridor chatting. He looks over at me walking up and he positions himself in front of the girl.

"Whoa cowboy, I got nothing against you, whatever is going on, I don't care but please man, don't hurt anyone."

"I won't. Has anyone come out of those doors?"

"No buddy."

I'm now directly in front of him.

"Here…"

I hand him a Glock, but he doesn't take it.

"…take it and take her and get somewhere safe. You see anyone who doesn't look right…

He cuts me off.

"You mean like a guy covered in blood who just took two guns from two cops?"

"…No, I mean someone who doesn't speak, have any expression, doesn't look like they have anything left upstairs and if they come at you, don't wait, just shoot."

He takes the Glock from me.

"You know what's going on, don't you?"

"Yeah. I do."

"Man…what is going on?"

"Trust me…take her…and go."

"…what about you?"

"The only thing I care about may already be dead on a table just past those doors…if that…"

I choke.

"...happens...it won't matter what happens to me."

He looks at her, she looks at him, and then they both look at me who just stares at those stupid fucking double doors that connect this corridor to another.

"My name is Sarah Rose, and I think Zachary and I are going to stay with you."

"Yeah, this is Sarah, Johnny."

I look at them, tears welling in my eyes.

"Why?"

They both smile and almost in unison speak.

"You look like you could use some friends."

I nod looking back down the corridor and then I nod, implying for them to follow me. I push through the double doors and Zachary and Sarah follow me.

I'm greeted by the sight of the doctor who took Jess, he walks next to a man who isn't a doctor, who isn't a nurse, who I recognize, who is now armed and pointing his gun at me quicker than I can get mine up.

"Put it down Valentyne!"

The doctor stops behind Detective Clayton who I'm ignoring and just staring at the doctors' scrubs, scrubs covered in blood, blood I assume that is Jess's. He looks at me behind that little surgical mask. Zachary and Sarah stand behind me, drawing closer. I don't raise my gun; it just limply hangs in my hand.

"Please Johnny. Just put the gun down."

"Is she ok?"

"Johnny please put down the gun."

"Is...she...ok?"

The doctor removes his mask quickly placing himself completely behind Clayton, he can't even look at me as he goes to speak,

"I'm so sorry...we did everything we could."

I drop the Glock and fall to my knees. I feel nothing but weakness at first, as though my body has finally accepted every wound I'd ever been dealt simultaneously and then the massacre continues on my nerves as all of that weakness converts to pain. I feel the pain of every hit, every cut, every electrocution, every burn and every bullet wound I have ever sustained rush back and melt away the numb. Years of torture, damage, and torment smothered suddenly by the feeling of heart wrench and inward suction, an implosion of my heart folding into itself. Each muscle in every section of my body clenches and I go limp. It can't be worse because what I am, what I fight for, what makes me, me, has just died. A long time ago, I wondered how a man could become a monster and now I know. I feel sickness and I'm absent from denial while combating acceptance. I can't breathe.

"Can...I...can...I"

I choke again and again as I look up at Clayton who holsters his gun and slowly approaches. I don't even feel it when Zachary and Sarah put their hands on my shoulders and squeeze. The doctor doesn't move. Clayton kneels in front of me.

"I'm sorry Johnny...I'm so sorry, I'll take you to her."

He helps me stand but I don't and Zachary and Sarah prop me up and all three of us walk down the hallway. They walk me up to the door of the surgery room and open it for me. I walk in and there in the middle of the room is an operating table surrounded by quiet machines and used surgical equipment and three attending surgeons who are cleaning the area up.

"Give him a moment guys."

Zachary and Sarah stand there holding each other waiting outside the room. Clayton stands motionless, letting the doctors pass him.

I walk slowly toward the table. I expect to feel the unreality as though I'll wake from a dream soon as I recognize this is just another one of my nightmares, but this all feels just like it is what I know it is, real. I stand next to the table looking down at Jess. She lays cold and naked with tubes running from her mouth to a breather and a nearby defibrillator is closer to her than I am. The table, the blankets, the bandages and all the gauze and all the areas touching her are covered in her blood. I slowly remove tape around the tube and then slowly remove the tube from her mouth and watch as her lips limply release it.

I didn't get to tell her I loved her before they took her to surgery.

She knew you did.

The pain fades as I hear that voice, I look back to Clayton who hangs his head and doesn't react to the voice in my head.

I look back to Jess. I just stare down at her. Every single memory of her seems to mesh and mold into the next and I feel the pain strengthen as it attacks me with the need to cry but I don't. It creeps across my arms and raises each hair. It twists my face and tugs my innards with illness.

I'm sorry.

"I'm sorry jellybean. I shouldn't have listened to you. I should've stayed home today. Even when I know it's not technically my home anymore. Home is where you were. I should've let this go or I just...I should've...I should've... killed them...killed them all before coming home...then I should have disappeared and never come back here...I should have just left it alone...left you alone to move on..."

My voice turns into a whimpering whine as tears snuff out my vocals and snot evacuates my nose.

"...I know I always say...I always say that...it could be worse...but what is worse than this?"

You could be dead.

I lean over, close my eyes, and kiss her. I close her lips with mine. I open my eyes, and I look into hers. I place my hand on her forehead and run it down caressing her face and then I close her eyes. I lift the blanket over her.

"It is time to go Johnny, I'm sorry."

I turn to Clayton, defeated. I walk toward him and turn my back. Zachary and Sarah look at each other and then watch as Clayton cuffs me. I can hear him read me my "rights", but I don't respond. Zachary tries to interrupt, pointing out this can wait, pointing out that I should help, and he should help, that there are bigger problems than me.

Clayton finishes and leads me out of the room. I stop in front of Zachary and Sarah and while Clayton tries to move me,

"Get somewhere safe, this is going to get a lot worse."

He nods.

I'm escorted out the corridor and down out the emergency exit and out of the hospital to the parking lot where Clayton's car is. The sound of sirens and commotion is deafening. I can hear people screaming and yelling in the distance. I can hear glass shatter, I can hear the looters; I can hear the car accidents and the howls of injury before they quiet, signifying the cessation of life. I look around in all directions and see plumes of black smoke snake up toward the heavens changing the color of the sky from white, to grey, to black. I am not a victim. I am the cause.

You could be the cure.

"Johnny, you know what is going on don't you?"

He opens the back door to his car. I look at him; look around and then with a single speechless nod, I get in the car. He closes the door and gets in the driver's seat, starts the car, and drives vigilantly through the surrounding bedlam.

MISSING TIME WITH REVENGE

Underneath an underpass, the smoldering and massacred wreckage of a once unique Camaro dies on its roof with its wheels still spinning and every fluid inside now bleeds outside on to the onyx below it. A single man approaches, calling out to the unconscious driver inside.

"Buddy! Buddy, are you alright?"

Greyor regains consciousness – *I say Greyor because I didn't wake up here, he did* – and un-straps the racing harness, falling hard against the ceiling, crawling over broken glass and climbing out; stumbling forward as he tries to fight the vertigo. The man who woke Greyor stands in front of a static black Kawasaki ninja zx-6r, which quietly purrs, idling.

"Yeah. I'm fine. The other driver...is the other driver, ok?"

Greyor points down the road behind them where three other cars have stopped, investigating the other vehicle, a destroyed cobalt blue ford F150 that lies on its side in a ditch. Greyor slumps over, feigning further exhaustion and injury.

As the man turns, Greyor stands straight and looks around for Sketch and his car. Greyor removes his boots and socks all the while watching ahead. The driver of the bike walks toward the wreckage.

With him in the distance Greyor jumps on the Kawasaki, painfully releases the kick stand, and throws the bike into gear, speeding off into the night. The bike's owner realizes and gives up a pointless chase, screaming for Greyor to stop.

Greyor shifts furiously from gear to gear reaching speeds that cause the landscape and all other vehicles to meld into a blur of red brake lights and bright headlights and his bike a single, straight beam, illuminating his direction through the darkness.

He passes other vehicles like a bullet in a blink of an eye and heads toward one place, with purpose. He and his driving defined only as: mercurial. The highway begins to split off; one way continues while the other leads off the highway on to a series of back roads with a hidden passage.

He takes the exit but doesn't slow despite the danger. These roads aren't perfectly paved asphalt; they are age-old concrete, ridden with deep cracks and serrated potholes, surrounded by untrimmed forestry. He doesn't slow down at all; rather he navigates each flaw magnificently keeping the same speeds only changing incrementally for sharp turns.

He zigzags down roads that don't look like roads until finally he arrives at a single stretch of asphalt that seems completely out of place, completely encapsulated by forest, in the absolute middle of nowhere.

He accelerates, heading down the road and as he grows closer to a distant structure bright halogens illuminate the night hidden in the tree canopy exposing him and this road.

The road becomes a key shape and borders a single parking lot but instead of slowing and parking he drives straight toward the main doors.

An alarm goes off piercing the silence of the night and he revs the bike as he grows closer and closer. He jumps off the bike and rolls onto a small patch of grass tumbling as the bike careens up the stairs and hits the doors, exploding.

The bike deflagrates, punching a hole in the double doors as its shrapnel cuts into the framework and stone. He is already standing, walking toward the doors with a gun in each hand. In his left hand, an HK USP .45 ACP and in his right hand: the famous M1911A1.

When his foot hits the first stair, he fires the HK USP at a guard trying to extinguish the fire that now eats its way in. He fires again, but this time, at the fire extinguisher that instantly and violently explodes outward, knocking two more security guards down and smoke-screening the entrance and extinguishing the inferno.

The fire dwindles harmlessly, and he is now inside. The recovering guards don't have a chance as they too are gunned down, both from an HK USP.

Four bullets down, eight to go with the HK USP. The M1911A1 waits patiently, cocked and locked.

Down the hallway spilling on endlessly are set after set of closed doors. The hallway splits off into two directions at its end.

The lights flash on and off exposing the hallway in a dim red for short second bursts before re-illuminating and then back to red.

The alarm speaker annoyingly pulses the same shrill tone over and over in short intervals that masks the footsteps of more guards approaching, but Greyor isn't listening, he's watching, just like the cameras overhead, that are now all pointed in the direction of his entry while someone watches him.

He can feel their footsteps through the bottom of his feet on the cold floor below, something he learned here, and he uses this to gauge their distance to him.

He pushes into a doorway not far from the split in the hallway as two more guards come around the corner with their weapons raised.

In the blink between the red glow and full illumination of the hallway he fires two shots in such close sequence that they sound like one ringing in the brief and short-lived stillness of the hallway he occupies.

Both guards drop, only a second apart before landing limply on the cold floor. Two fresh casings roll closely to each other as Greyor moves from that doorway to the next.

When he gets close to one of the guards, he pulls the man close and retrieves his access card before moving on. He gets to the split in the hallway and stops. He pokes his head out, quickly glancing, and sees no one to the right, so he pulls himself back. He ducks and looks out again but this time to the left, no one. He slowly walks out, pointing his right hand down the right hallway and his left down the left hallway, a gun for either direction.

The hallway to the left leads to the living quarters, where he lived. To the right, the entrance to the courtyard, and the many rooms he was tortured and trained in. He turns his attention to the left and walks quietly, calmly, and attentively; still ignoring the alarm and the flashing lights.

Vigilantly, he passes each closed door looking momentarily in through each plate glass window. Each room has an occupant sealed tightly behind an electronically locked door.

He feels the steps of several people moving down the opposite hallway, he turns walking backward toward the door at the end of this hallway. He drops on his right knee and takes aim closing his right eye, lifting his left hand. His finger squeezes out the last six rounds of the HK USP .45.

Five men fall at the other end of the hallway while one remains standing, and he opens fire. Greyor pushes from the ground and pins himself against a doorway watching rounds tear into where he was a second ago and he watches the spray crawl toward him.

He drops the HK USP .45 and lifts his right hand and takes aim, exhaling. The guard falls, spraying rounds from his MP5 into the ceiling as blood jets from a puncture in his neck where his artery used to be intact. The casing ricochets loudly and slides across the hall bouncing from the wall Greyor's hand touches.

Greyor rises, his gun never leaving its direction: the end of the hallway the guards just came from. He puts his back against the last door and slides the access card through. He hears a voice on the other side of the door and pushes through. The voice comes from a man, who tries to run to the other side of the room to a door, and he is screaming something into a phone,

"He is here!"

Greyor lunges at the man, catching him by the back of his coat, pulling him backward on his ass. He turns the man around and shoves his gun against his face,

"Hello Hanson."

He looks up whimpering,

"Greyor. Please. Please don't kill me."

"I bet this is how powerless she felt."

"How who..."

Greyor smashes his gun against Hanson's jaw, a thick jet of crimson sprays out across the floor of this room, almost reaching the chair that sits in front of a security station. Greyor lifts Hanson to his feet and leads him to the chair throwing him on to it.

"Turn off the alarm and open my room."

"Greyor…"

Greyor pushes the gun against his forehead,

"I'm not going to ask twice."

Hanson swivels in the chair and pushes two buttons, the first stops the pulsating alarm and the flashing lights, and the second opens a room in the hallway Greyor came from.

"Give me the medication you gave Riley."

Before Hanson speaks Greyor taps his gun against Hanson's forehead.

"It is in my lab."

"Where are the twins?"

"Out looking for you."

"Take me to those pills."

"No."

"No?"

Greyor heaves his gun hard against Hanson's jaw in the same place he struck moments ago.

"You're just going to kill me."

Greyor points his gun at Hanson's thigh and fires. The bullet cuts through the chair he sits in and digs into the floor followed by a ravine of blood and as Hanson screams, he jams the barrel into his mouth smothering him.

"I'll do it now if you want?"

With a smothered gurgle Hanson whimpers a 'no' and a 'please'.

Greyor lifts Hanson and pushes him through the door he came from with his left hand on his collar and his right hand pointing the M1911A1 ahead of them.

Hanson reluctantly pushes his feet into the floor as Greyor pushes him. His feet drag, smudging black lines, leaving an inky trail behind. They move past where the other patients or "prisoners" are kept and down the hallway quickly but suddenly Greyor stops them. He looks at his room or what he and I refer to as our "cell" and stares at it.

"How many more are here that are like me?"

"None of them are like you."

"You know what I mean."

"No, Greyor, I don't."

"How many of them are here against their will, when they had a will?"

Hanson doesn't speak.

"How many guards are left?"

Hanson looks around and forces out his sentence.

"How many have you killed?"

"Eleven."

"I'm not telling you. Keep in mind you just answered your initial question."

Greyor forces him forward and begins their journey to his lab.

"Which question is that?"

"No one here is like you."

Greyor doesn't respond.

"You don't get it do you? You can't be anyone but who you are. Look at what you do. Witness your ability. You were born to do this. You have no regard for who you kill; no remorse for the lives you extinguish. The most troubling thing is: you're a brilliantly efficient and..."

"Shut it."

Greyor whips his pistol against Hanson's shoulder and continues to force him. They push on past the living quarters and through more and more electronically locked doors until they arrive at his lab and when they do Greyor tosses Hanson violently through the freshly opened door. Hanson skids violently across the floor before smashing into his desk. He tries to stand but Greyor lifts him and forces him down on it. He pushes the gun into Hanson's nose.

"Pills...and Hanson?"

He looks at Greyor wide eyed and questioning.

"I'm not going to ask again."

Hanson looks at him as if to argue but suddenly the fight from his eyes dissipates and with a sigh he points to his desk and taps on it.

"Get them."

Greyor releases Hanson from his grip but not from his sight; his gun still pointed at him. Hanson fixes his shirt and coat from the wrinkling of being tossed around.

He limps dragging a trail of blood behind him from the wound in his leg. He almost falls but he catches the corner of the large blue steel and polished glass desk.

He turns to look at Greyor who seems pale and exhausted. He can tell he is wounded but still somehow very aware of every move Hanson makes.

With a blank stare and repositioning of Greyor's weapon, Hanson opens his desk by entering a code on a transparent keyboard build into the desk. The drawer flies open, and Hanson goes to reach in.

"Whoa."

Greyor walks around the desk and brings his gun across Hanson's face, batting him bloodily to the cold bare floor. Greyor sees the pills first, but he also sees the pistol.

"Thought so."

Greyor looks down disappointingly at Hanson. Hanson likewise tries to look up at Greyor, but he's disoriented and losing consciousness as he sits in a pool of his own scarlet, soaking, and watching his life slowly leave as it expands across the white floor.

"Get up."

Greyor demands.

Hanson groggily tries to respond.

"I can...can't."

Greyor takes the pills pocketing them; exchanging these ones for his old ones as he throws his pill bottle in the drawer, closing it.

He lunges at Hanson, ripping him to his feet, throwing him toward the door they came from.

"I'm not done with you yet."

Hanson can barely stand but Greyor helps him, digging the M1911A1 into his lower back, carrying him by the collar. When they return to the living quarters Greyor leads Hanson back to the control station but stops suddenly as he passes the one place that you can't open from the station.

He stands there motionless with Hanson hanging by his coat. He shakes his head. He thought he heard something: whispers.

He looks down the barren hallways.

He looks at Hanson.

He hears his name again.

He looks at the room that is never open. The room he's only ever seen the inside of once: the room with the tank, the tank that holds a man.

Greyor looks to the room and then pulls Hanson toward it. Hanson can barely keep his eyes open and has barely said anything since his lab. When he realizes where they are going life floods back in, waking him.

"Greyor, what're you doing."

"Open it."

The panic overwhelms his voice, cracking it to a higher pitch before crushing it to a whimper.

"Greyor. No. Whatever you think is in this room...whoever you think he is...he isn't prisoner...he isn't the answer...your answer. You can't let him out."

"Hanson, open the fucking door, now!"

Greyor throws him hard into the door, once, and then again, and again until finally he pleads for him to stop.

Hanson's face is mangled, displaced, completely twisted and bloody. His glasses broken into shards and the frames painfully protrude in his skin, almost completely imbedded in his face.

Hesitantly, Hanson places his hand on the door controls, and it reads his fingerprints. It beeps and then requests a password and Hanson gives it.

The doors slowly open and Greyor walks in forcefully dragging Hanson who has found the last of his strength, powered by fear, fed by adrenaline.

"Greyor, please, stop."

Hanson screams as Greyor tosses him into the monitor station.

Greyor stands for the second time in wonder, staring at this large ancient tank. Someone inside somehow calls to him. Greyor raises his hand, in it, the gun and aims it at Hanson's head.

"This is how it started…"

Greyor points with his free hand at the tank.

"It started with him, didn't it?"

Hanson stays quiet.

"Whatever he produces helped erase Johnny and create me. Like Silk, he produces something, naturally."

"Greyor…you don't…you can't understand. Nothing about Ian Hane is natural…you need to leave…you can leave. You got what you wanted. Just leave it alone. You're free. Letting Hane out won't do any good."

Greyor knows Hanson is genuine in this one and only moment, terrified by the man trapped in that machine. For some reason beyond Greyor, beyond me, he wants him to be out. As if Hane calls out for help. Greyor isn't convinced despite Hanson is out of reasons to lie, he knows he is dead, if not now, soon. Greyor adamantly barks.

"Hanson, let him out."

Hanson rises from the ground with the last of his strength with tears streaming down his face with a begging and drooling expression of plea.

Greyor's expression doesn't change. Hanson begins to type away on the keyboard bypassing safeguards and entering code. All the while he begins to talk continuing some foreign procedure on the computer.

"Greyor are you familiar with the story of the Pied Piper?"

"What?"

"It is a story where a city is infested with rats and the Piper; a ratcatcher, says he'll rid the city of the rats for payment. The city agrees and the piper rids the city of rats with his magic pipe. The city doesn't pay him, so, in retaliation he does the same thing to the children, he leads them away never to be seen again."

Greyor looks at Hanson questioningly.

"What does that have to do with Hane?"

Hanson stands at the terminal, and he has finally stopped working, waiting on Greyor. His finger rests on one key but doesn't press it.

"Hane is the Piper."

"What does that even mean?"

"You'll see."

Hanson presses the key and steps back. The tank shudders violently as the rivets loosen and it sounds as if something unlocks.

Several closed portals on the lower side of the tank open, evacuating some strange fluid thicker than water on to the floor.

Greyor steps away in disgust from the approaching fluid. Hanson stands in it, shuddering. The tank stops shaking and then the room goes quiet. Another noise and a hatch on the tank springs open.

Greyor points his gun at the hatch.

Ghostly white hands smack on the hatch opening, followed by arms and then a head.

Ian Hane pulls himself from the tank.

His baldhead covered by a strange metallic cage and his chest encapsulated by a stranger apparatus. His skin is sick and transparent, void of color to the point where green snaking veins are visible as are muscle movements.

He wrenches himself out and weakly slides off the tank, crashing painfully to the floor. The wires and tubes that snake from his skull and chest retract suddenly as he removes the mask and apparatus.

He takes a deep inhale as he opens his eyes and mouth for what appears to be the first time in a long time. His movements are incremental as he slides himself to a sitting position and even in his apparent vulnerability; he hides some sort of strength, some deeper confidence. He looks from under his hairless brow at Greyor and smiles hauntingly.

Greyor doesn't smile; he just goes to aim, closing his right eye. When he fires though, Hane doesn't fall back dead, but Hanson does.

When Greyor opens his eye again his arm is pointed at Hanson, who now falls limply to the ground with a gushing head wound. Greyor turns his aim back at Hane and goes to fire, but can't.

"I know that gun. That gun has tried to kill me before. You changed parts of it, but it is the same weapon." He looks at the weapon in wonder.

Greyor furiously tries to pull the trigger. His hand begins to shake violently at first, and then his arm, and the shakes seem to move into his shoulder. He throws his other hand on the weapon trying to help pull the trigger but now he just rocks back and forth.

"You picked that gun, why?"

Greyor says nothing as he painfully persists in his futile attempt at shooting Hane.

"Put the gun away."

Greyor without thought or want quickly holsters his weapon.

"Help me up."

Greyor again, without physical hesitation, lifts Hane to his feet. When Greyor touches him, he feels sick, as he smells the decay. Hane looks at Greyor who now closes his eyes, and with a disgusting grin he reaches up and touches Greyor's face.

"Now we're both free."

When Greyor opens his eyes, he is standing in his room, his former cage. He spins around quickly, and the door is wide open. Outside the room the hall is quiet. He doesn't understand how he got here. He doesn't know how long it has been. He goes to the hall and all the doors are open. He walks by rooms, and they are empty. He stops questioning and starts moving. He knows he needs to deal with these injuries before he loses control and gives it back to me.

He goes back to his cage and grabs clean clothes, a pair of boots, and a medical kit. He heads to the shower room.

He walks the halls of Southstone that are now abandoned and silent. All the while he is still prepared, always vigilante, always waiting for more enemies but he knows there are none here, at least for the moment.

He walks through the doors of the shower room, and he remembers Riley and now I do. He remembers what happened here.

To him this is the shower room where he found liberty and knew her name was Riley, but to me it was just another bathroom.

He removes our black dress jacket slowly exposing the scarlet scabbing mess that is our shoulder.

He throws on the hot water and goes to a nearby cabinet removing a large metallic bowl.

He opens the medical kit and removes disinfectant, emptying it into the bowl. He dilutes it with hot water. He takes a towel and soaks it.

He patiently wipes the crimson mess from the area. He doesn't feel the sting. He removes the needles and stitch thread from the medical kit and begins to close the wound from the front first.

When he finishes, it stops inking scarlet. He sits down on the bench and turns toward the large L-shaped mirror and begins to awkwardly stitch closed the entrance wound.

When he is finished that he turns on the shower and removes our destroyed dress pants. He washes the wound on our thigh and then stitches that closed too.

He hops in the shower and is out as almost as quickly as he got in. He throws on the clean dress pants and clean shirt leaving it open around our neck. He throws shaving cream on our face and shaves without the guidance of a mirror because it is completely fogged. He does it so accurately that it doesn't nick us or snag on stubble; clean and quick. He washes our face and then wipes it clean with a towel drying it. He tosses on the holster and a clean jacket and even a tie. He turns the tap on hot and begins writing on the mirror.

I know what he is writing because in this memory I'll read it soon enough. He throws on socks and then the boots tying them neatly. He reaches into our pocket and pulls out the new pills and pops two. He turns off the hot and then turns on the cold. He drinks several large gulps of water and takes a deep inhale. Bringing his hands to his face and he closes our eyes.

Now that I remember this, I have one question and one concern: What happened to the rest of my bullets and whose side is Alrick on.

I mean, if these pills don't inhibit memory, did he know that when he took them from me?

CAPTURED

"Johnny, please state your full name for the record."

"Clayton, look around, you think your law matters right now? You need to be with your family, protect what you love before someone takes it..."

"Johnny, please."

I sigh and sit up. He turns the recorder on.

"My name is Johnny Raymond Valentyne. I was born February 14th, 1984. I've killed so many people that I have lost count. Some deserve it and some didn't. The people I killed that didn't, I killed under the identity of Greyor Allblack, forced to by a company known as Grim Associations. I killed these people so Grim Associations could use fine print to collect their claims and get rich. I now know that it probably wasn't just about the money. What is happening right now is their doing and I don't understand the point but they are behind it. They have released the medication into the general public somehow. It is changing anyone who takes it. I'm not sure of its entry or delivery but I know that drug and it is doing this...

He said something about how he would show himself one day. Something along the lines of show himself to the masses..."

"What?"

Clayton interrupts me, tearing me back from my thoughts. I look up from the bleak cold table and my galvanized bonds tear the skin away and choke the circulation from my wrists.

"Ian Hane."

"Who?"

I see his unease. He is distracted by the chaos outside and trying to gather what he should do with me.

He looks outside our room, an interrogation room. Four greyish-white walls each sound proofed and heavily insulated. On opposite walls: one doubled sided glass mirror and one heavy polycarbonate glass window fortified by bars. From outside that window, he focuses.

He can see the failure of his law. He knows today isn't the day he should be interrogating me.

He knows that what is happening outside is much more dangerous and present then the defeated man sitting across from him.

"What did he mean by that? Did he mean this? And even if he intended for this one day, how could he have orchestrated it from within that tank?"

I'm barely giving Clayton any attention. I'm bouncing ideas of myself.

"Johnny?"

My attention returns.

"Yeah?"

"What are you talking about?"

"A man named Ian Hane."

"Who is he?"

"I don't know but he was in a strange tank at Southstone."

"A tank. What? Where is Southstone? What is it?"

"It is the facility Grim kept me in. Me and others like me. It is where they make the medication causing this. I believe the medication to be made from something that comes from Hane. Something he produces causes this effect."

"This isn't science fiction Johnny, people are dead."

"I know. This all sounds like bullshit but I'm telling you the truth."

"Johnny. I want to believe you. I do. Really. You have to give me solid evidence; something I can use."

I point outside.

"Explain that."

"I don't know what is happening Johnny and you apparently do, but you have to help me understand."

"I already told you. I don't know. I don't have the answers, and we don't have time for this."

He messes through his blonde fuzz that springs from his crown, once neatly kept, formed and cropped but now messed from exhausting patience. He takes a deep breath and then looks back at me.

"Anything, give me anything: a name or names?"

"Grim Associations."

"Clean."

"Benjamin Sketch?"

"Doesn't exist."

"Then who did you find in the rubble of my old house?"

"Couldn't identify the body."

"Henry Alrick?"

"We're still looking for him."

I sigh, rocking back, looking out the same window he is. I look back on my wrist, back at my bonds. I'm attached to a bar protruding from the table. I'm barely able to reach my face. I smother my eyes in my hands and pull at my cheeks before looking back at Clayton. He sits forward.

"For the record, let's start from the beginning. Tell me what you remember."

Somehow, I tell my story. Even so I'm always distracted by what is happening outside and what just happened less than an hour ago.

I detach myself and spin him the tale of my life. I tell him what I remember of Southstone.

I tell him what they did to me and made me do. I list the people I remember killing. I iterate my time as Greyor.

When I arrive at how my day started when I realized who I was and how I survived the massacre at Charlie's, he's gone white.

He sits up, adjusting his collar as I continue and removes cigarettes and a lighter. He briefly interrupts me, offering me a cigarette and lighter.

I flash a forced but sincere smile, accepting. I pause to light it as I look outside.

I see the streets. They have been closed off by swat vehicles; a newborn perimeter separating the station from the congested city blocks that surround it with a single-entry point that is swarmed by police, armed to the teeth.

They escort people in a bottleneck through a gate checking each and every person that comes toward it.

I then notice from a couple blocks down a horde of people approaching the barrier quickly. That is when the shouting starts. I hear officers on a megaphone barking for the "rioters" to slow but they don't. The door to the interrogation room bursts open as a man in a suit flies in, sweating and panting.

"Clayton lock this guy up; we have a big problem."

I look from our intruder to the street. I hear the canisters of gas careen through the air toward the mass. I hear the gagging of weapons. Clayton unlocks me. He lifts me up and as we leave the room I hear the deafening sound of heavy gunfire. Which is quickly drowned out by screaming and shouting, and then the thunder of stampeding. The mass reaches the barrier as the door shuts behind me. Clayton escorts me down a hallway toward lockup. Cop after cop runs by strapping on body armor and loading weapons.

"Clayton, look what's going on, you can't lock me up now."

"Johnny, I'm sorry, I really am but I have no choice. Regardless of what is happening, I can't let you go."

"Clayton, please."

When we get to the holding cells, he opens one and brings me in. He sits me on a bench and locks me to a new bar, connected firmly to the wall.

"I'm going to take your cuffs off, please don't make me regret it."

"You're not my enemy Clayton, I realize you're just doing your job but reconsider, man, look around, you won't have a job soon."

He goes to his pocket for the key, but something knocks us both over. An explosion somewhere outside or in resonates through the building, completely rattling it, shaking the entire foundation. The lights flicker as Clayton stands.

"What the fuck."

He looks at me while I try and rise, I hold my arm up, signifying for him to unlock me. I go to speak but the sound of my voice is drowned out my shouting, gun fire, and what sounds like hundreds of people running through the hallway. Clayton pulls his gun instead of the keys and moves to the opening of the cell.

"Clayton!"

"Johnny, I'll be back, you'll be safe here."

He steps out aiming down the hallway and disappears. A few moments later my cell door closes. I hear him shout for someone to stop. I hear running. I hear him fire unloading a clip. He shouts. I hear a struggle and then silence, absolute silence, and then the sound of feet again, at least ten different sets coming down the hallway.

"Clayton?"

A group of people smash into the bars staring at me and reaching for me. Each one them, expressionless, void of any apparent humanity, absent from any former identity. When they recognize they can't get through they run back down the way they came. I'm left with silence and my thoughts, which circulate on the one desire to wake up from this nightmare. This can't be happening.

I pull at the cuffs and the bar attached to the wall. I heave again and again but nothing budges except for the skin on my wrist peels away in flakes, and starts to turn red. I scream at Clayton. I scream for someone. I hear nothing, so, I continue to try and free myself. I kick the wall near the bar. I tug and pull over and over again at the chain. I call out for Clayton again. I repeat everything. The attempt to free myself, and pointless cry for help, I do this repeatedly until I pass out. Then I wake, I do it again and again, nothing. As the days go by inside my prison, it gets quieter and quieter. Just outside these walls, in the city, the screams get louder and louder, and this goes on for days, until one day they begin to dwindle, and then nothing after. The silence has spread from inside my cell to the decaying city beyond on it, and I'm left completely alone.

HEART IN A CAGE

It has been nine—no, wait—ten days, maybe longer. I don't know. I can't keep my eyes open or my head up. I'm so weak. I've been sick several times and I tried to keep it far enough away, so the smell doesn't make me sick again.

I'm locked to this wall. My wrist is numb. There is a deep crimson, almost black bruising wound around where the cuff is. The skin is pulled back, crusted, and scabbed. My skin is pale and clammy, covered in a layer of sick sweaty film.

I'm so thirsty. My mouth is completely absent from saliva, so dry, I can feel my sandpaper excuse for a tongue flicking against each dry ceramic chiclet; things I used to call my teeth. The broken ones are decaying and rank; I can smell their sickness.

My voice is completely gone, I can't even muster a whisper; my mouth is too dry. I think I'm going to die here. When you have been locked to a wall for this long without food—or more importantly water—you don't have the strength to try to escape because you have already used it when you still had some. I have lost my strength and my voice.

I exhausted it by nearly dislocating my arm. Yelling to the point of a guttural howl for someone until my voice was so strained it disappeared. Battering and smashing my knuckles in a useless attempt to weaken galvanized steel of the cuff and destroy the chain, futile.

I can feel myself accept defeat. I have tried everything to free myself but even if I got free of the handcuff I am still behind bars. I am going to die in this cage. I slowly reposition myself on the bench—which takes me several minutes—all in the effort to make myself more comfortable but I just fall, slumping over oddly, almost hanging from my chain.

Day and night have become a blur as light and dark come and go quickly as I fade in and out of consciousness. Neither feels as if they stay long enough for me to tell time.

I feel moisture. I taste water. My face feels wet. I pry my eyes open, but I don't move because I can't. I gasp as rainwater falls on my dry skin rolling down my cheek into my mouth. My mouth slowly takes on moisture. I can feel it calm my swelling gums. It washes over my tongue, and I slowly begin to create saliva and with it, strength. I actually have enough energy to sit, so I do. I sit up and lean my head back and let dirty rainwater spill down the wall into my mouth.

I form a smile, as I am relieved. The storm outside is so furious it forces its way in. I hear thunder now and the sound of rain. I just sit and drink. I don't move from this position until I hear something from beyond the thunder.

I hear footsteps echoing from outside my cell, coming loudly down the hall toward me. All I do is turn my head and look at the bars.

"Hey, Johnny boy, wow, you look like shit. How long have you been in there? Surprised to see me?"

I exhale but I am not relieved nor am I afraid, I just can't talk, so I just breathe. Silk stands proudly holding a device I don't recognize in one hand, leaning into the bars and then pulling back after he smells the stench I can thankfully no longer smell.

"Oh Johnny, that is horrible."

He looks at my makeshift washroom which is only a couple of feet from me because I stopped being able to get myself to the toilet. So, on the way to it is a sick mess of shit, piss, and vomit.

His nose scrunches and he pulls his onyx locks back and across his forehead before retaking his posture. He looks down the hallway and nods at someone I can't see or hear. The cell opens and he stands in the place of where the bars were, between the cell and hallway, but he doesn't step in.

Groggily, and with nothing short of difficulty, I try to hold my head up to look at him. He crouches, placing down that object, and removes something from his belt at the back of his pants pulling out his black dress shirt. He cringes momentarily, wincing from a hidden wound, and then he smiles at me patting his stomach.

"Recognize this?"

He waves a 9mm Glock at me and I immediately know that 9mm Glock. I know an object has no humanity, but I despise this individual pistol. I recognize it is just a tool; just a gun but I know what that gun did. I feel a little bit more strength return.

"I'm sorry for what we did to you Johnny but consider this a gift. Mercy even."

He goes to throw it past me but to his surprise and mine, I catch it from the air with my right hand and with some foreign strength, speed, and accuracy, I turn it toward him and fire. Nothing. A chamber-less click and the slide opens back, signifying the gun is empty. He falls backward,

"Fuck! Man, am I glad I didn't load that. Shit...how...you never cease to amaze me, Johnny."

With that, my strength is gone as the pistol now weighs a ton, and it and my arm fall hard against the bench as the gun spins from my hand, falling to the floor. My head falls back, and I try to cry, defeated. Instead, I use what little strength I have to smash the back of my skull against the wet wall, and I look back at him with water in my eyes.

"Awe. Johnny. I'm sorry. Really, I am, I hate to see you this way."

I wince and then look away.

"Here, I'll do you a favor."

He removes a single round from his pocket and throws it onto the floor. As it rolls past me, he speaks again but this time his words are muffled and seem distant.

"Do what no one can seem to do to you Johnny and kill yourself. I know you always say it could be worse, you could be dead, but really, would death be that bad at this point?"

He stands up with a visage of sympathy smothered by relief. He feels certain that this is my end, and I think he may be right. With a single word, I stop him dead in his tracks. I have asked this question so many times and for so many different reasons, but today, this time, for the first time, he tells me truth. The question I ask is: why?

He doesn't turn to face me yet; instead, he looks at the person who is beyond my range of sight. He signals them to wait, and he turns to face me. I lift my head and from under my unwashed brow, with my eyes fixed on him, wide and lidless, I repeat my question,

"Why?"

"Have you not put it all together yet? I thought you remembered everything?"

I don't nod or respond because I don't know, remember or not, I don't know why.

He looks disappointed and annoyed and before he speaks, he rolls his eyes.

"Once you go all black you are not supposed to come back, but you did, and so did that waitress and I can only assume it is because of these…"

He shakes the pills I left Henry so he could "get a taste of his own medicine".

"…And of course with the help of this batch of medication, you remembered the life we stole from you. But what you obviously don't understand or remember is that you stole mine first, well, our situation, is like the age-old question: who came first, the chicken or the egg..."

Silk smiles a smile that I would give anything right now just to remove it with my fist.

"...You of course remember Laurie...Yeah...from that look you're giving me, of course you do. Well, she was one of our first policies, and yes, I carried it out, but you probably put the two together by now..."

He makes a jerking motion and then throws his hand open, fingers spread and palm empty, like he is tossing something from it. This is his: "I fucked her to death gesture."

"...She didn't die of a drug overdose, let me tell you that. Now, with the best intentions, she made you her beneficiary but before we could even wait the appropriate time to approach you, you found us. Yeah, that's right; the drug den you raided wasn't making just any old popper. We were making the first batch of those good old grey or all blacks. The day you killed poor innocent Billy Kade, and killed your way into our house, I had the misfortune of running into you for the first time, face to face..."

He waits for my reaction. I can't give him any, but I'm incrementally satisfied in the immediate recollection of breaking his nose because he is the only one of those guys I didn't kill, however, that satisfaction is quickly stolen and turned into unending regret because I could've prevented all of this happening, and from stealing my life and others. Maybe, with his death back then, I could've stopped everything before it started. I get sick with this thought, but nothing comes up because I have nothing left. No tears, words, or contents to evacuate, not even the strength too, if I had any.

"You broke my fucking nose, killed my friends, blew up my house, and if that wasn't enough…you stole my fucking girlfriend. Yeah, Jess. She was the first person, fuck, still the only person I could be with physically that didn't die, and you fucking took her from me. To make everything so much worse, you didn't die, and she fell in love with you. She fell in love with you and completely forgot me. I never forgot her, and you bet every fucking dollar in existence I never forgot you…"

He points to his face, which is my face, smiling my smile.

"Eye for an eye, you took my life, so I took yours and yes, I lived it, at least as long as I could…"

I want to speak. I want to scream. I want to call him insane and question why he did it, but in some sort of way, I understand why, I don't understand why I do, but I do. I completely grasp his sick obsession to get back what was lost and easily agree with his justifications in doing what he did. Like it or not, hate it or not, I get it. I may hate the ends, but I completely comprehend the means.

I understand better than anyone the need to get their life back and as long as one can get it back, no distance exists because there is no going too far.

"But like everything around Johnny Valentyne, nothing lasts, except Johnny Valentyne. By the time I looked like you, the company was too big, and the drugs were too important. I didn't even get to see Jess, but I did keep her and your friends alive, so I had a fallback plan, a way out. I kept them off Grim's radar and made damn sure none of them touched anything that was laced with the grey or all black drug. I was going to leave Grim when Hane went into the tank, but as always, you fucking ruined that. You started acting up. You, despite the impossibility of it, began to remember and behave like the man you were, and I couldn't chance you coming back. So, I tried to speed up the process and get you killed but no matter what I did, what we did, you wouldn't die. So instead, we tried to capitalize on that quality, and I stayed around to oversee it, but everything backfired...

So now, instead, I'm going to kill everyone you love, and completely erase you and rebuild. This city will be a memory because no help is coming. No government and no military. They are going to burn this place to the ground just to prevent this from spreading. They think it is viral. They don't have a fucking clue. We destroyed the landlines systematically when this city started to lose control, and with these..."

He holds up the device that I didn't understand but now do. The device is a police issued frequency jammer, and when activated, blocks cell signals in a one-kilometer area. With enough of them, they could stop any signal from getting out of the city.

"...Every cellphone that isn't ours, is jammed, and can't call out..."

As he rambles like a villain in a bad movie, revealing the sinister plan, I stop listening because I am too weak to care or do anything to stop it. Within that thought, I feel something open up from within me. Like a wound, scabbed over, but torn over and air washing over it and into it, this feeling starts to intensify incrementally, massing exponentially by the second. I don't know what it is; but it can't be what it feels like, because it feels like hope.

"She was the only one Johnny, and you stole her. Sorry to sound cliché… but if I can't have her, no one can, not you, or that idiot she was with, the one who killed her…"

He pauses for air and reflects before continuing his confession.

"…I really was going to start over. Not everything I told you was a lie, not everything I showed you was a fallacy. They wouldn't let me leave and neither would you, so plan B. Always have a backup plan and then have a backup plan to that plan. My plan involves the very large sum of money the company has earned and to take said sum to a new city far away and start this again. I have Henry and with him I can make more of both drugs. After the military burns this city to dust, no one will ever know but I'll know that you and Hane are ashes. The bomb has to kill you, both of you. Even though you both never fucking die, but this will do the trick, it has to…"

He stops, ponders, and he wants me to grasp a concept he knows that I can't, and he revels in this, and finally, he continues.

"Oh, sorry Johnny, don't you know? Of course you don't…you woke up the fucking devil. You think Sketch was bad; I'm bad? Hane is the most venomous of all of us. People throughout time, Hitler for example, could spin words like webs on the minds of many, and have them stick and stagnate. Hane is as bad as Hitler was, but Hane is better at making people do horrible things without reason. Free will is void when he speaks. Before the meds, he was the control. However, age was killing him, so he went into that tank, and we manufactured the poison he produces, mixed with Henrys wonderful memory erasing drug, and we sold it to the masses hidden in everything from birth control to antihistamines to over-the-counter regular strength headache relievers. While that monster slept, things were better and much less insane. We made it better, so we left him locked in that fucking tank. You woke him up and let him out and if the bomb doesn't get him, the world will have to pay the piper...that is if he gets out, which I doubt he will..."

He takes a deep breath, catching his breath, and I have leeway to process all of this, which I doubt will make a difference.

"No more company to control me, and more importantly, no more past coming to kill me. No more Johnny Valentyne, grey or all black, Ian Hane, and no more fucking Grim Associations. Just Silk Crisante, fantastic, and free. I'd love to forget you but sadly, until I get this fixed..."

He points to his face, my face.

"I won't. Goodbye Johnny. Thanks for nothing and don't worry, if you don't have the balls or the brawn to kill yourself, this place will be particles in less than one hundred and twenty hours. Give or take the hours gained or lost by the protest of people trying to find another solution aside from incineration. Of course, I wouldn't count on it, because this is a problem they can't get close enough to identify. So goodbye Johnny and good fucking riddance."

I watch each step as he exits, I watch until he is gone, and he has left my cell open because he is sure I'm dead. I feel my strength leave and my eyes forcefully and exhaustively go to close, but one thing keeps them open, and that is the bullet that rolls back and forth on the floor in front of me. Overwhelmed by further foreign strength, I dive from where I am sitting and rescue the bullet, ignoring my left arm, and how it has just popped free from its socket. I painfully wrench backward with the round in my hand. I chamber the bullet and close the slide, and I point the gun at what I assume is the weakest part of the chain: where the chain and cuff meet. I take a deep breath in and then I begin to squeeze back the trigger, exhaling, while my hand shakes to keep the target. The bullet tears from the barrel and the bullet hits exactly where I wanted it.

It deflagrates on the steel where chain meets cuff and with the impact sprays of chromatic blue and yellow sparks shower down. It sends an unimaginably painful vibration up my arm that feels as if it is separating bone and flesh as it goes but it is just a feigning reaction to the impact.

The show and pain give nothing, as the cuff stays solid. I try to make a sound as I fold off the bench and weakly tug at the brace with my feet planted on the bench, I heave backward. Whimpering, I pull with the very last grain of strength I have that comes from my core, as if I saved this one last attempt knowing it would render a wanted result, but it offers the same as all of my other tries, nothing.

I try to move but I just sit there, staring. I try to avoid hopelessness, the pain. I attempt the idea that if I rest, I can try again, and the link will be weak enough to break. I know it won't. I know this is it. I think of my life. Everything lost and remembered that led me to here. I recognize how unsuitable this is as my end and how unfair that I never got what I wanted, not even close. Everything I loved, taken. Everything I fought to get back, gone.

I wasn't the best person, before the company, before losing myself. I was never happy with what I had. I didn't make the best of bad situations and because of that, more bad situations were born. I didn't appreciate Jess while she was a part of my life, even then, I lived in the past and the past led me right here. Jess was always good to me – no – she was amazing to me, and I got her killed. I cry aloud, weeping, tearlessly. She believed in something that wasn't – at least in my opinion – wasn't worth believing in. I didn't see it then and I struggle to see it now, and I remind myself that is why I'm here, trapped in this fucking cell.

She loved me, and what we had, but I couldn't drop the horrible things that had happened to me and the things that continued to happen to me back then. She was always right, and I should have believed in myself because maybe then, when the money came, I wouldn't have accepted it, and I wouldn't be here. This is the only thing I go over and over in my mind about. My choices. My ability to blame myself, or inability to love myself, blame myself or not, I don't deserve this, no one does. I realize, in my selfishness, I am responsible for the deaths of many I love. I could go over this, in my mind, how I could've done things differently, but it wouldn't matter now, nothing does.

I can't produce tears because I'm so dehydrated. I can't move either. It could be malnourishment, or it could be hopelessness but I'm still just fucking staring at the cuff. I can't feel the gun that I know is in my hand, I could see it if I looked, and I know it is there, but I won't look away from the cuff and I don't have the energy to lift the empty gun.

I stare at the cuff for an hour and my eyes close without my help, shutting without energy to keep them open. I feel myself giving up and preparing to die. I am so exhausted and worn down. I have nothing to fight for, no purpose, and no love. I consider if I die here that everything, I did to get back would be for nothing but then again, everything I came back for is either gone or it will be soon, and I'll be left with nothing. I know who I am and what I've done. I also know, I can't live; knowing the things I've done offers no reward. I'm better off dead, this is finally the end for me...

Don't you fucking say that...everything we did to get back here and you're going to give up? Let them get away with what they did to you. Did to her. No. Get up and get free. We. Are. Not. Done...

Great, just fucking great, now I'm crazy. I'm dying and trapped and now I'm losing the only thing I have left, my mind. This voice screams out in my mind, something I've never heard, and I recognize it isn't there. It is just sickness, thirst, and hunger playing with my reality.

No, you know exactly who I am. Are you going to let Jess rot? You are one of a few that know what is happening and if it gets any worse, the utilities are gone. Now, ask yourself, do you want Jess to rot in some hospital morgue? Or burn in a morgue, if and when they drop bombs?

It dawns on me that Jess is lying in the hospital morgue, naked, and if this chaos persists, her body will in fact rot, or be incinerated if Silk is telling the truth, and I can't let either happen. I feel something surge through me. Power and purpose somehow return to my shambled state. I deny my weakness. I do not understand how but I effortlessly, but painfully tear my left hand through the cuff and free flesh as though I could've done this the whole time. Then again, it could just be the thirst, the hunger, and the sickness causing rapid weight loss so I could free myself. That seems more likely. Now I just have to stand up and get out of here.

I'm going to bury the girl I love. This isn't how I die and that isn't how she will rest. She will not rot in a fucking morgue because the power went out. She deserves better.

I rise, slowly; incrementally inching upward as though I am walking for the first time and technically, I am walking for the first time since I've been locked to that wall. I stumble forward falling hard on my knees. I gag but I have nothing to vomit so I shake it off and stand.

I make it to the bars and rest. A whole ten feet and I'm already too dizzy and I feel unable to persist. I stare at my hands that are dry and cracked. My wrists, swollen and bruised, the blood dried and crusting on several crescent shape wounds from tugging at my cuffs. With my right hand, I find my lips with my fingers, and I realize they are so dry, and completely cracked, speckled with blotches of dried blood. I hold myself up, waiting for the dizziness to leave.

Come on Johnny, ten more feet, or at least walk into the hall.

Shut up.

I move from the bars slowly, practically throwing myself from the open door into the opposite wall. When I hit, I look down the hall, and I see rubble and bodies. Each cell is now open, and the hall is barren except for the rubble and buried bodies near the guard station. I go to speak but I still can't talk.

I slide myself along the wall. Slumping into it, using it as a support, because my legs feel like mush. My muscles are weak and unused. My body aches numbly, but it feels almost like it isn't there, I feel detached from my body as I push along the wall. Shaking from the weakness and propping myself up as I dizzily focus.

The pale walls are unforgiving, cold, and colorless and because of the same pigment, I can't see the end, as it seems to bend around and go on endlessly; I'd be lost without the rubble and damage. I remind myself, I'm sick, hungry, and fatally dehydrated and more than likely hallucinating.

I can't determine if what I hear is actually there or it is just my mind playing tricks. When I reach the rubble, I slump down and rest.

Unknowingly my left-hand rests on the face of a corpse. I don't react; I just stare at him. I know him or should I say knew him. It was Clayton's partner. He stares back at my jaw dropped. He didn't die in an explosion. He is covered in debris but that isn't what killed him. He was beaten to death. His gun sits empty in his hand. The slide pulled back exposing the empty barrel. I sit up against him and look down my next challenge. The next hallway. I can't smell his decay and maybe I'm lucky. I squint to focus. I hear sounds again. I question if they are there. I sit back and rest. I don't know for how long but when that strange force returns; my sudden and unexplained strength, I open my eyes.

I stay still because someone stands at the end of the hall. They don't move. They just stand there staring. I play dead or rather, mimic my company. I sit up like Claytons dead partner and stare down the hall. My eyes however aren't glossy and sick white. I still have color. I'm still breathing. The person at the end of the hallway robotically turns, looks back at the hallway they came from, and disappear down it.

I push up with my back against the wall and force myself forward. I don't get far as I stumble into the pale wall to my left and slide down it. I use it to support my slow journey. I stop every couple of feet and listen. I hear a dying siren. It pulses out a shrill cry and it seems to be at its end. Blaring out the last of its life and with every burst the gap between the next becomes longer and longer.

I reach the end of this hallway, and it veers two ways but in the middle of it is an elevator. I thumb the button and lean into the doors. I think back and try and remember when Clayton brought me in. Push past the pain and smother the memories that will lock me up. I need to focus. I need water. I don't need to find the sorrow that waits for me. I'll find it and welcome it but not now. I pull together the few things I remember.

He brought me down several hallways into this elevator and with the elevator, he brought me down to this floor. I remember walking by some sort of recreation room or lunchroom on the way in. I want to go there. I know if I can get to the ground floor; if this elevator even works, I will find the room with sheer necessity of hunger and thirst. It'll lead me there. I hear the elevator come down. I also hear the sound of feet hitting the ground, running rapidly, and drawing near.

I feel the sensation of people coming. I turn my head and from one hallway, I see shadows down one hallway, cast largely around a corner, growing rapidly closer in the pulsing light of the alarm. I don't move. I just lean into the elevator doors, hoping they will open and swallow me before whoever is coming gets here. I know whoever is coming wants to kill me. They are like the ones from the courtyard at Southstone. I saw them. I saw them at the bars of my cage.

Those shadows become people. People spilling around the corner void of what makes people, people. My finger taps the button on its own, nervously, repeatedly, pressing it inward.

It seems most moments in my life feel like an eternity. They seem to stretch on much longer than they should or maybe it's my perception; the way I see it. Most times things seem to slow down, and I am forced to absorb every detail. Most times this works in my favor but sometimes it doesn't. Some moments linger and stretch out, like realizing loss, and being trapped in the instance it happens. This moment falls into that category.

Helpless, I hammer the elevator button, which does nothing to assist the descent, I know this, but I don't stop pushing it in. I hesitantly look over, down the right hallway from the mouth of the elevator. My throat sinks dryly as I watch the crowd spill down it toward me, fleshly rolling closer, trampling each other. Uncaring, one moves off another like a stepping ladder, throwing themselves closer. When they're within thirty feet, I see it, that expression. The identical look on each of their faces. The absence of humanity that I'm so familiar with. The ferocious apathy of hunger coats each of their retinas, pinned open and exposed by their leathery tired lids. Their faces bruised and covered by scarlet, a reward of passage from pedestrian to murderer. Without control they have killed following their instinct, compelled to do so by a drug they unintentionally took. They don't sleep. They won't bargain. They don't want to talk.

They want nothing more than to kill each other or more importantly at this moment, me. The closer they get the fewer they get. Their numbers diminish. There are ones who stay behind and wrestle and writhe in feud and don't move forward until they claim the life of another. The successor of the bout rejoins the swarm that intends to consume me.

Open. Please fucking open. If you don't open, I'm dead. I can't – yes, I cannot – defend myself. They have found symmetry in their step, guided and unwavering, and they are now fifteen feet from me. Ding: a sound that isn't just a sound, it is my life being saved. The button light goes dark, and the stainless-steel doors open exposing an empty elevator. A single flickering light exposes a solid oak interior and a strange grate-like pattern on the floor. I fall in and turn. This time I push a button that does something. No delay. No wait. When that button is mashed down, I fall forward, and the doors slide to close just as the first of the group reaches me. I expect disappointment but I'm greeted by a single blank stare, empty brown eyes, tenantless. I somehow smile as I select the ground floor.

I know I'm not out of danger because I have no idea what or who waits for me on the ground level and with that thought, my smile disappears. This time that ding brings fear. When the elevator stops on the ground level what is left of my stomach sinks further and I do my best to stand. The elevator doors slink open.

The hallways are blackened and torn a sunder. White walls peeled black and broken exposing the foundation behind them. A fire tore its way through this hall, possibly a flash fire. Debris litters its mass. Furniture misplaced and toppled and melted. Unrecognizable corpses burnt crisp statuesquely haunt the floor. I count ten as I stumble out doing my best not to fall.

The decay is masked by whatever explosion tore out the upper levels. I see sunlight at the end of the hall and turn away from it. I move as quickly as my frame allows. I wander, almost aimlessly, through the leftovers of a once proud and strong police station. Around several turns and at the end of a hall near processing I find the room I'm looking for, the break room.

I open the door and fall in, shutting the door behind me, quietly. This room nearly untouched only coated by a new layer of dust and completely undisturbed. I go to the water cooler and kneel. I open the valve and drink down gulp after gulp of water. I get sick, turn away, and vomit water into a garbage can. I go back to the cooler when my stomach stops twisting. I drink a little bit at a time this time, allowing my body a chance to recover. I feel my strength return, not completely, but enough to stand without shaking. I go through the cupboards and fridge and gather the only food that isn't spoiled. Beef jerky, raspberry pop tarts, and oranges that surprisingly haven't gone bad. I eat a little at a time. It is an effort to chew and swallow but I get the food down and thankfully keep it there. Little by little I feel my strength return. I pull the table in front of the door and everything I can find to block the only entrance to this room: the center table, eight chairs, a side table, a bulletin board, and an air hockey table now completely cover the door.

I gather the food and lie down in the center of the room. I close my eyes and sleep. Time seems to fade. I sleep hours away. They melt away as my eyes close and open to the change between night and day. Every time they open and close, I feel better, at least physically better because when I do wake, I taste salty tears. I recognize my misery but give it no attention I distract myself with the food and water when I wake and then return to sleep when I've had my fill.

From slumber to consciousness, I continue. I check my wounds, and I keep time by how much they've healed. As time passes, I occasionally hear sounds from outside the room or maybe they are outside the building. I have slowly moved further and further away from the door. I now sleep directly in front of the opposite wall. I know the next time I shut my eyes when I wake up, I have to leave because as always, time is against me. The bombs didn't drop yet. I find several more hours of sleep and I dream for the first time, in a very long time.

WHAT HAPPENED TO HENRY ALRICK THAT NIGHT

Henry's eyes flick to the clock hands watching them pass. He knows what is supposed to happen, but he doesn't know how it begins. He's seen it take hold of countless people. He's watched, horrified, as their identities disappear hauntingly and violently. He hopes that his transition will be quick and eventless. The time is gone. He closes his eyes to the sight of half an hour passing. Nothing. He doesn't feel disconnected, rather the opposite, he has never felt this connected. He considers his metabolism. No, he has seen this work faster on people with a slower metabolism. He opens the pill bottle and spills one capsule into his hand. A slight smirk turns smile and corrects the grimace as he sees the small numbers that give this drug its own identity.

The sadness, gone; completely and totally replaced by joy. This is the drug the company took from him, the drug that he spent his entire life trying to manufacture but never knew he succeeded in creating until right now. He throws the little miracle back in the protective case. He grabs his keys and goes to the door, but he stops hard as he sees a silhouette and hears the hollow echo of its step.

He turns and runs toward the window trying to open it. Its archaic design offers several issues. It's stuck and brittle and cannot be opened quietly. He tries as hard as he can to open it as quietly as he can. It opens a crack as he feels the night seep in cooling his fingers.

He hears the footsteps, so close, right outside his door. He gets the window up a little more. The knob noisily wiggles. The window opens a little more. The nob gyrates loudly, followed by a knock. The window wide and breathing, and Henry, relieved, begins to climb out. He almost falls on his ass, as he's torn quickly back inside and thrown savagely into his desk. He looks up to see his human obstacle and immediately recognizes—or should I say thinks he recognizes—me.

"Johnny! Please don't...listen..." Henry cries.

"My name isn't Johnny." My doppelganger says smirking.

"Greyor?" Henry questions, wondering if I lost the truth in the last hour I left him.

"Wrong again." My copy joyfully responds.

"I don't understand."

Henry tries to stand but the guy he thinks is me, puts his foot on his chest and gently pushes him back against the desk.

"Henry, where is it?"

Henry looks at him, feigning the fact he knows what he's talking about, hiding his horror. The man asks again but this time without words, just his eyes, his static clay eyes ask by themselves.

Henry knows how important it is to hold on to these pills. He knows he has to protect these pills as if they were his only child and the only child left in the world, his baby. He can't recreate this formula. The specifics are unknown to him because he has formulated this drug over and over and over again and the company holds all of his work. The only thing they don't have is the original formula, how he synthesized a pill that created me, and others like me. This specific combination was an accident and as soon as they found out it existed, they stopped his work. That's when I came in and began to take them apart.

Henry digs into himself and finds what we all have buried but rarely unleash, courage. In one sentence he allows something to live that all the while has waited and this is its moment.

"You can't have them."

"I'll just kill you and take them, don't be stupid."

"You can't kill me. You know as well as I do, they can't make the drug without me."

"Henry, we are past that, we have everything we need from you. Well, except that drug. The one drug you're not giving me."

Henry feels the bravery seep away and out from every pour in the form of cold sweat, dribbling down every crevasse. He doesn't want to be here. He wants to hide. He wants to run. That sweat instead of running stays still, and stops dripping but does not dry, holding and pooling in little droplets waiting for something. Henry and his sweat don't know what. The man, impatient, waits for something, something like for Henry to hand over the pills. For Henry to speak. For Henry to try to move the foot he has pressed on his plexus, but Henry doesn't. Henry is petrified, collapsing inward, and trapped by choice. Fight or flight. Try and run or stay and fight. Henry always chooses the first and never the latter and that is why Henry is always and will always be under their thumb.

You're wrong.

Henry quickly and surprisingly—so quickly and surprisingly my double and I don`t expect or see it coming—throws his weight upward. He lunges, punching, landing a hard straight punch into the stomach of my chameleon winding him and more. Henry doesn`t even anticipate the result. My clone falls hard into the window, cradling his stomach suspiciously because as hard as Henry hit him, he knows it wasn't as hard as he wanted to; something is off. The hit was hard, but Henry has never been in a fight and that took every ounce of strength he had just to get his foot off. Henry rises and runs toward the door but is stopped by a plea.

"Henry...wait...It's me...Silk." Silk cries out, completely dilapidated by agony.

"Silk?" Henry finds comfort, relief almost, in his claim, even in the impossibility of its truth.

"Yeah. It's me."

"Why do you look like Greyor?"

"You mean Johnny? He isn't Greyor anymore."

Don't believe him Henry, he's lying.

"They did this to me. They needed him locked away because they can't. He is out of control."

"I don't even know what is going on Silk. I thought we had a system. The insurance, the system, it was meant to fund my research, finally, when I find the perfect combination, they cut me out...why?"

"Henry, they never intended to cure those people. They never wanted a cure. They wanted a medication that would erase people, populations at time. The insurance just moves the same money. Over and over and over again. The insurance fraud helps chunks of it disappear and reappear without anyone asking questions. They wanted control. They wanted doses and you gave it to them. Doses that would stay hidden and finally when the complete version was administered everyone was empty, like the subjects at Southstone. Those pills you have are the only mistake they made..."

"No..."

"Yes, Henry, why would they produce that much for so little control population? You knew...you had to have known!"

"No...I didn't...I thought...I thought it was about the insurance...the money...I didn't..."

"Yes, Henry, you did. You knew since your initial funding, you knew that no one would fund some wild medication trial, especially a drug that did the exact opposite of its intended purpose. You knew that Lennox, a fucking drug dealer, was the only one who would loan you the money or help you. Somewhere you'd have to know. He's gone now Henry and so is your medicinal prototype. Grim wasn't founded or funded to steal money. You chose not to see. Give me the pills Henry. I can stop this."

Don't Henry. He's lying.

Henry watches Silk rise, gripping the bloody mess that is now his shirt. The seeping wound reopens. The truth, if only Henry knew, is bleeding out in front of him. In Henry's face you can see it he wants to run. Instead, he walks toward Silk, afraid. Silk smiles, my smile, but it isn't mine. Henry grows closer and closer. Silk stays where he is, sure of his control, sure of his power but Henry stops and asks the one question I want to hear.

"Why do you look like Greyor used to? Why do you look like Johnny Valentyne?"

THE UNAFFECTED

Zachary runs without breath, without end; sure, of the fact that if he stops, he is dead, and so is she. He carries Sarah. Not in his arms but with one hand.

He pulls her down a desolate alleyway. An alleyway completely unlike what an alleyway is supposed to look like. No turned over trashcans or thrown about trash that has formed rot or birthed maggots. No stagnant puddles or rigid and crumbling potholes. No cardboard homes empty of their tenants. No walled in dead end that abruptly appears around a corner. Granite interlock: possibly travertine, goes on foot after foot laying this alleyway. This pathway laid and imprisoned by onyx painted ten-foot fences with gates that lock electronically. This alley they run down runs between expensive condos, which were perfect to live in until they heard the broadcast that told them that no help is coming, and now Zachary and Sarah are without direction trying to escape a place that once protected them.

A group of mindless, formally civilian, now emotionless, "affected" follow as their steps echo thunderously, almost dreamingly, at their heels. Zach turns suddenly, sling-shotting Sarah in front of him, firing the Glock I gave him, which he didn't use until today. He squeezes out the last of the clip, dropping three "affected" before turning and running; comforted and (only slightly) by the fact that he has slowed and reduced their numbers.

Zachary and Sarah come around the corner of the alleyway and freeze at the sight ahead on the open street behind a wide berthing, open gate of the endless black fence, exposing them to the chaos that crawls across the main streets. No longer encapsulated and protected by the massive housing complex; they stand exposed with "affected" closing in from behind and a horde that isn't aware of their presence yet.

Beyond the street and its writhing naked and savage occupants, a group of unaffected roams unnoticed. They intend to escape the city and its limits, search for help from the outside and beyond. They, like me, unsure of this being localized or global continue their slow and precise escape. One stops and points across the "affected", silently identifying these people are like them, unaffected.

Zachary and Sarah move again, darting out into the open street, followed at first only by their initial pursuers. The "affected" don't scream or signal others. They don't begin to rally together.

They don't identify only Zachary and Sarah; instead, they join the war that takes place in the street. Eerily and mutely clashing with each other, occasionally grunting when pain is felt, but completely void of expression or concern. When one kills one, one attacks another, and so on. They group too large to notice numbers dwindling, immediate or long term. The almost complete population of the entire city, here in the streets, mindlessly raping and killing each other; reason and restraint don't exist. Mercy doesn't exist and from this sight, looks like it never did.

The nine other unaffected: Manny, Max, Aila, Salina, Tanner, Jen, Brand, Tristan, and Shawn watch in horror as Zachary and Sarah run through the army of affected. Max looks at Manny who leans on Salina, his color fades, and he is soaked in sweat.

"Salina, take the others and go, I can't leave those people out here."

Aila shakes her head tearing, and pulls at Max. He scratches his shaved blonde skull and pulls his hand down over his strong gold goatee. His face turns her expression from concern to comfort.

"Babe, I promise, I'll be right behind you guys. Just go."

Brand, Tristan, and Shawn take to Max's side. Tristan smiles, lifting a brown brow, and puts his hand on Max's shoulder.

"We're coming with you."

Brand taps an unlit smoke on his knuckles and blows on the filter. He sighs, lights it, and looks up at Max.

"Don't argue we don't have time."

Max shrugs and gives Tanner a look of judgement and expectance.

"Get them out of here."

Max gauges his shotgun and looks at Tristan, Brand, and Shawn.

"If we're going to do this, let's make it quick."

Max kisses Aila hard on the mouth and winks as he turns and runs back the way they came from. Brand shrugs, hands his gun to Tanner as if relieved to rid himself of it, and chases Max.

Tristan checks his .357 Magnum and spins the chamber, counting the bullets, and locking it in a loaded order and follows Brand.

Shawn, flushed, leaves his pistol with Manny, taking a baseball bat from Tanner. Shawn isn't upset or bothered by risking himself for more survivors. He is sick and sad that he couldn't save the one who mattered most to him. Shawn joined the party after Max rescued him as he fought back affected after losing his love to their violence.

Shawn and Rebecca were unaware of the situation as they left their place that day. They had spent several days in bed cementing their affection. They didn't answer the phone or watch television. They made love, ate, showered, and repeated that for almost a week. When they left to go meet up with friends that they had plans with, they were attacked.

Max had been driving around gathering anyone he could find and bringing them back to his house. Shawn couldn't keep Rebecca from them. He wasn't a stranger to violence, but he wasn't prepared to kill people. He did though. He killed several before they overtook him. He was being pummelled, and if Max hadn't have stopped and helped him, Shawn would be dead. A part of Shawn didn't want to be saved. A part of him wanted to find that same group of affected and kill them with his hands, with nothing but his hands. He wanted to feel them die.

Shawn, revisiting this horrible event, follows Max, Tristan, and Brand impatiently awaiting the opportunity to kill affected. He knew these were innocent people somehow turned monstrous, but it didn't matter, he couldn't wait to kill them. They had changed, and so did he, the frightening difference, still unrealized, he, unlike them, made the choice to change.

Tanner and Jen go to Manny and Salina, helping them lift Manny down the alley. Aila, looks back, while following the group.

They arrive at the large stairs to the transit tunnel. A thick red steel portal borders large glass doors. Tanner gives Jen Manny's weight and draws his Glock. He soundlessly instructs them to wait and opens the doors. He walks slowly down each large concrete step. He listens while walking down, waiting for noises besides his, in the emptiness of the declining staircase, vigilantly glancing from the steps to the end of the staircase to prevent a loss of footing.

His hand shakes, nervously, as he glances back to the doors and returns his sight to the last of the steps. When he hits the ground level, he looks down the large glassed-in hallway and stops dead in his tracks.

A single man walks toward his direction, unaware of his presence. He lifts his gun and takes a deep breath, aiming. The man walks slowly, still unaware of

Tanner. Tanner's shaking gets worse; he can't tell if this guy is affected. He can't risk killing someone who isn't, and he can't risk the noise from firing his gun.

"Hey!"

Tanner cries out, his voice cracks, sounding almost pubescent. The man stops, without startle, and calmly looks at Tanner. He sees Tanners gun and lifts his arms in defeat.

"Please don't shoot."

Tanner sighs and lowers the gun.

"Are you alone? Are you being followed?"

"Yeah. I'm alone." The man says,

"Are you being followed?" Tanner repeats, raising his voice slightly, returning strength and confidence to it.

"No. I'm not. Are you alone?" The man reflects Tanner's emotional state.

"No, I'm with survivors. We're getting out of the city. What's your name?" Tanner enquires sincerely, lifting the demanding rasp and replacing it with friendliness.

"My names Laflamme. What's yours?"

"I'm Tanner. Wait here, I'll get the group."

Tanner runs up the staircase leaving Laflamme in the hallway. When Tanner is out of sight, Laflamme smirks, removing a cell phone, and begins to text someone...

Zachary slugs a man in the face with the empty Glock, dropping him. He kicks a woman who tries to choke him, tossing her backward, knocking several more affected down with her. Sarah punches a girl who looks like a teenager, but could be older than eighteen, who kicks at Zachary's back. The could-be-teen falls, holding on to Zachary, attempting to drag him down. They both move backward, keeping the affected in front of them. More and more start to run at them and they are running out of free space as they are being forced toward an electronic store.

A large man leaps from the group and spears Zachary into the window of the electronic store. The glass shatters in a hail of shards, raining down over them. Sarah jumps in the store, tearing free of the hands that try and pull her back, groping at her frame hungrily. Luckily for her, because of the small entrance, the only space into the electronic store is now fought for by most of the group that occupies the sidewalk in front of it. Zachary knees the large man in the ribs as his hands look for Zachary's throat. The large man falls off as Sarah runs past him and he lunges at her ankle. Zachary kicks from the ground and runs after Sarah, stomping on the man's wrist, helping free her. Zachary and Sarah run through the still and dark isles of the electronic store heading to the back, searching for an exit. The man lifts himself, following them, followed by others who now spill into the broken portal of the building. Zachary and Sarah locate the shipping and receiving doors and push through them into a large warehouse. They run by scaffolding isles filled with cardboard boxes and brand-new electronics mummified in industrial saran wrap. They can see the bright red exit sign in the back of the warehouse, and they speed up despite the burning of their exhausted lungs and limbs. When they get to the emergency exit and smash down on the metal bar that opens it, they hear the swarm enter the warehouse.

They push on through the emergency exit, afraid, and unaware of what waits beyond. They come out into the night on large concretes stairs that fall down into an open receiving alley, wide enough for trucks to bring new items to the wide receiving mouths of the stock doors. Either end of the alley opens to the street, already congested by affected who now turn their attention to Zachary and Sarah who sprint down the stairs.

They head toward the less congested side, running full on toward a mostly empty side street. Before they get even a foot away from the stairs the emergency doors burst open and ten affected flood from the doorway, some of the first even fall of the railing, dropping and landing painfully in the open alley, crushing bones.

Sarah pulls Zachary as he tries to fight off a man that stands in their way. When they get around the corner, into the side street, they're greeted by five affected who now charge them. From behind, the ones who aren't broken, fight their way toward Zachary and Sarah. Hopelessness washes over the tired frames of Zachary and Sarah as they now back toward a fence. A woman jumps at Zachary as he places himself in front of Sarah, he tries to throw her off, but she hangs on. Sarah violently hooks her in the jaw, drawing scarlet. A man grabs at Zachary as he struggles to shake the woman off. Zachary lays into the man, crushing his nose, but he doesn't fall. He grabs Zachary by the arm and pulls Zachary into him. He brings a fist down and catches Zachary in the eyebrow. Sarah kicks at the woman, finally, disconnecting her from Zachary but she recovers and now clings to Sarah, taking her kick as a challenge.

Two more men run in and try and bypass the guy Zachary is already fighting off. The man on Zachary brings another hit down on him, almost like he is hammering a nail with his fist, primitively. Without accuracy the man brings his hands down on Zachary like an ape smashing the ground, asserting his territory. Zachary steps back, through the pain and hungry hands, and he kicks upward, clipping the caveman in front of him in the chin. Territory claimed. Warm blood jettisons the man's mouth as he bites down into his tongue, toppling over. He falls between the two affected men who lunge at Zachary. Zachary steps back into Sarah, separating her from the woman, and pins Sarah against the fence, completely protecting her from the two men and woman that now attack, tearing at them with hands that they use as paws. They try to rip free his clothes and find flesh. Zachary now wildly throws out punches and kicks trying to prevent the terrible things that will certainly follow if they get him pinned. Behind them more flood in. Zachary kicks and swings but they are now forcing over him.

Zachary closes his eyes, swinging blindly as he is quickly overwhelmed. He has lost hope as now all he can feel is pain and the hands of those who cause it, he goes limp, and prays that he can stop what is coming for Sarah as long as he can giving himself over to them, and with letting go, all hope leaves him...until he hears the shotgun blast and is painted by the blood of those who attack him. His fight quickly returns, shortly followed by hope.

The two men and one woman who were on him are thrown backward, suddenly and violently, like rag dolls tossed across a room; their remains tossed to the ground as they explode in a hail of ball bearings and hot crimson, shredding them dead. Another loud blast cuts through the group behind them, and a third blast cuts a large path between them and the mass of affected.

Max gauges out the empty shells from his shotgun while running toward Zachary and Sarah. He turns the gun, flipping it into a bat, and knocks a man over. One-man lunges at Max but is dispatched by a thunderous clap as a magnum round cleaves his chest wide as Tristan takes his place, covering Max. Brand and Shawn clear two more people. Max signals for Zachary and Sarah to follow him as he falls backward, turning the bat, back into a shotgun as he fires into the crowd that now runs in. Brand and Shawn help Zachary and Sarah, pulling them backward.

The group run toward a slung open set of doors to an apartment building. Max covers the front and Shawn covers the rear. As soon as the group is inside and running toward the way they came, Shawn stops. He brings the baseball bat up and swings hard catching a close affected, breaking his jaw. He falls, sliding bloodily and stays motionless. Another affected is greeted by the freshly painted end of the wooden Louisville slugger. A sick pop drops a female affected with a freshly cracked skull. Brand stops running, realizing Shawn isn't with them, and he turns.

"Shawn. Let's go." Brand cries from the other end of the hall.

Shawn ignores Brand and waits as more affected pile in. Shawn pulls his black skinny jeans up, which are held together by patches and thread, and tightens his belt, resting his bat under his armpit. One comes through the doors and Shawn punches him in the face so hard his fist tastes teeth. Shawn recovers his bat and stabs it into the man's throat viciously. As the man recoils, and his throat collapses, Shawn leaps up, swinging at the man's head, his swing contains such force that it looks like it will decapitate him, and nearly does, crushing his neck. When Shawn's Converse heels touch the ground, the man lands limply, gushing blood from a cavity across his skull. Shawn goes to move outside, out toward the affected, but is pulled back into the building by friendly hands. The door closes and locks shut. Brand throws Shawn into the wall.

"What're you doing?" Brand yells inches from Shawn's face.

"Let me go. I want to go. They have to fucking die...I'll kill them...all of them...let me go Brand...let me go." Shawn manically screams, flailing, trying to throw Brand off, but Brand holds on.

"Those are people Shawn, sick people, they don't know what they're doing." Brand pleas, his voice rings with reason or at least attempting reason, not completely convinced of what he is even saying.

"No. Those aren't people. They were people. Keyword, were, and no longer are. Those people are just animals." Shawn cries, calming, tears welling in his sad eyes, his anger fades, replaced suddenly by sincere sorrow.

They both jump as they hear banging on the doors; they walk backward as the banging becomes pounding. They both jump immediately startled by the hands on their shoulders.

"Guys. We have to go. Now." Tristan says, empathetically joining the conversation, bringing an unarguable and reasoning clarity. They listen to him as though he is the only one who knows what to do. Tristan doesn't seem phased or affected by the situation. They know he doesn't know what is going on or what to do but he has a calming confidence that they all believe. Tristan motions with a single flick of his peppery hair in the direction of the group, and he smiles, a smile that seems completely out of place because it doesn't belong here or near anything like this.

Max stops in front of the apartment exit and looks out the empty walkway looking at the large red steel transit entrance. The walkway is empty and undisturbed. He opens the doors and keeps low, indicating for others to follow in the same fashion. Tristan, Brand, and Shawn re-join them and keep the same pace. They all stop to where Max initially noticed Zachary and Sarah. Max motions for everyone to get low, just like last time when he watches, they watch. He watches and points at the mass of affected who have stopped fighting and now stand still.

"What the hell are they doing?" Zachary asks rhetorically taking his place next to Max.

"By the way, guys, I fucking owe you one, I love you." Zachary smiles, jokingly, looking at the rest of his rescuers.

They all confirm him and Sarah, even just for a moment, all of them are just glad to see another person with life left in them, and they all laugh, without sound, smiling sincerely, even though momentarily, they immediately return to the reality.

"Do you think they are coming to? Do you think whatever this is, is wearing off?" Brand questions hopefully.

"No, this is something else." Tristan says, getting closer to the fence.

The thousands of affected that fill this street seem to stand absolutely still, statuesquely waiting, as they all turn and stare synchronously in one direction. From quiet to deafening, sound rolls closer, and closer like thunder. The group of survivor's watches, confused, and terrified, as the affected seem to part. Biblically they separate like the Red Sea supposedly did. The opening grows wider and wider as the affected walk backward in perfect unison. From the mass, one-man walks, alone, followed by the eyes and bodies of each affected and from behind him, thousands of more affected drone's march. That man isn't like them, he is animated, and his expression is that of dominance. He is six feet and ageless. He doesn't look elderly, but he doesn't look young. His skin is the color of the sky before a massive thunderstorm, grey, and his eyes are milky white, cold, and dead without color, or pupils or retinas. He wears a once white, now mostly red dress shirt, riddled with holes and tears, covered by a weathered, bullet hole riddled, black dress coat and matching black and worn dress pants. *He is wearing my dress shirt, the one she gave me, the one I abandoned at Southstone, more than that, he's wearing fucking everything I left at Southstone.* He throws up his collar on the jacket as though he's cold. He runs his hand over his hairless leathery head and looks up. The affected stop and turn their attention to what he looks at. At first the sky but when he looks elsewhere, they look to the same place.

Max rises from his knees, fully standing, and starts heading to the transit doors. Everyone else follows. They ignore the sequenced eyes of the operated affected who watch them. Speechless, expressionless, and nearly motionless each of the affected follows every move the fleeing unaffected make. They all share and try and shake the fear as the situation has gone from chaos to order.

The man points in another direction, not toward the survivors, but somewhere else. Somewhere back into the city core. They begin to walk, in order, assembling perfect lines. They walk past the man who stays back and watches the group. The massive army moves back into the city, back towards the place he pointed, that place is the police station I'm unconscious in. I know that this isn't a dream and that it can't be what it is. I want to wake up…fuck that. Want left a long time ago; I need to wake up. Then like the first pound of a bass drum in a silent and empty studio, a voice explodes in my mind, foreign and terrifying.

"Wake up Valentyne, I'm coming." The man, Ian Hane, whispers.

GOTTA GET MY GUN

I wake up from my "dream" which I know couldn't be a dream. I'm not sure how I saw what I saw. I'm not sure what I saw was real, but it felt that way.

Who are you kidding, it was fucking real, you know it was, he is coming.

I'm not sick or weak. I get to my feet, and I feel my strength flood back in quickly, flooded by purpose. I need a gun. I need my gun. I have so much going on upstairs but have no time to deal with it. Here I am, again, confused, but not bleeding out but cities away from ok. I don't have anything to go back to, but I have something else, I need to stop this. You know the saying: "It's going to get a lot worse before it gets better?" Well, right now, that is just about the only thing that makes sense to me.

I start to move my makeshift barricade, exposing the door. I stretch quickly and check my wounds. They've healed slightly but nowhere close to how healed I need them to be. I'm comforted by the idea that I manage to come out on top usually even how injured or unaware I am. That is good enough for me. I need to get my gun and any weapon I can find and get out of here. I know where my gun should be. It should be stored in evidence with the rest of my belongings. I need to find the evidence room. Start small and build. That is what I'm going to do.

I open the door slowly and soundlessly. I peek my head out and swing it, checking both ways, no one. I walk out and shut the door behind me. The sound of the mechanism finding its home, signifying the door is shut, throws out a noise that I didn't want. I hear movement somewhere, but I can't determine where. I head back to the elevator. I don't know where this room is, but I doubt they would keep an evidence room on the main floor.

I get to the elevator and push down the button. Surprisingly, the elevator doors don't open. The elevator has moved. I'm not an expert in elevators but I'm pretty sure if no one uses an elevator it remains on the same floor it last stopped at. I could be wrong. I hope I am because if I'm not, these affected people can operate an elevator and when it gets here, I have to fight for my life. I look around at every direction before looking back to the little guide that tells me what floor the elevator is on, and it is almost back to the main floor. I step back, preparing myself. The elevator arrives. I raise one hand, ready to punch and another ready to defend. The elevator lets me and anyone else on this floor know it's here, and not so conveniently, that I'm here too.

The doors open. I lunge forward. I stop. No one is in the elevator. I relax and start to enter when I'm hit hard from the side. A former police officer turned bloodthirsty psychopath is on top of me, punching me. He isn't a cop anymore. He is a product of this chaos. Without expression or understanding he hits me with the intention of murdering me. He doesn't even know he is missing an eye. He gets three more shots into my face and body before I reactively defend myself. My brain and body don't seem to be in the same place because I can't take my attention off the empty bloody hole in his skull. I put my right hand on his face and with my left arm I guard myself to the best of my ability from his strikes that painfully pound my flesh. When my right hand finds that cavity, I dig my fingers into it and toss his head into the elevator opening. I get out from under him and throw his head back into it. He continues to fight as I smash his head into the doorway. The elevator makes a loud shrill noise signifying the doors can't close. Fuck. Die. Die already. I dig my fingers deeper and grab his belt over his back with my left hand, smashing his head harder with the entire weight of my body.

All the while the elevator continues, calling out, probably recruiting more affected. I question how this guy is still alive, and I know as the texture of the skin around this wound is charred. He didn't bleed out because whatever took his eye also cauterized the wound. I let go of his belt as he smashes his head into my face. I fall off and he gets on top of me. Fuck. He throws a solid hit into my eye. Figures. I close that eye as I feel the surrounding socket swell. He hits me again. I bring my arms up and use my elbows to shield each hit. He is now straddling me. When he goes to grab my arms and remove them, I throw an uppercut into his chin and as he rocks back, I lift him off me. I pull him into the elevator. Wildly, I try to push a button while throwing him back against the elevator wall. The doors begin to close but are stopped as his foot falls out, blocking them. I can now hear people running outside the elevator, down the hallway, toward us. Fuck.

I kick him hard, and he falls into the wall again, but this time I leap on him, pulling him further into the elevator. I pull his tie up from under his tactical vest and wrap it around a support bar in the elevator, knotting it. I let him go and mash the door close button.

Again, through the closing doors, I see the haunting expressionless faces of more affected. When they close, before I get to pick a floor, I feel hands around my neck, and I curse out loud before my voice is cut off from his choking arms. He is free and on my back. I throw him and myself into the wall behind us as hard as I can. A sharp pain as his forearm finds my Adam's apple. Lightheaded, I try and get an arm under his forearm, but he squeezes with uncanny strength. I throw an elbow into his ribs, but that Kevlar vest pads the blow. I'm losing strength without air. I go to his belt, searching for a weapon, and I find one. Of all the weapons he could have on his belt, he has a taser. I step down with the last of my strength because if I don't get air, I'm unconscious. I crush his foot under my steel-toed boot. His grip forced slightly to relax, and I get my arm under it, and I taste air. In floods back my strength and I return another blow to his foot but this time much harder, changing his balance. I get my arm under his forearm, and I slam us back into the wall. I escape his arms, tearing the taser free, moving from him and turning. I fire. The probes bury into his eye socket and release massive current into his skull as

I hold the button. He drops instantly, as his other eye sickly pops, exploding. Fresh blood and ichor leak down his face and with it, he's dead.

I fall back and look over my shoulder at my choices for elevation. It has to be on one of the lower floors, somewhere secured, but away from the prisoners of course. So b1 is out of the question, so it has to be b2. I push the button down, greeted instantly by the dim red light of my selection. I push the trigger of the taser, nothing. Battery is dead. Fantastic. I look to my eyeless dead company and throw it back to him. The elevator stops and I take the same position before the door opened, ready for another fight even when I'm really not. The doors open and I'm nearly blinded by light, impenetrable halogen bulbs brightly light this hall. My eyes adjust and a directional sign greets me, listing every possible direction. Records ahead, evidence to the left, and armoury to the right.

"Thank you, my inanimate friend, I appreciate the direction." I chuckle, slightly comfortable in this hallway.

I walk down the left hallway; I keep quiet, sneaking each step softly forward. I know I should go right; I should go to the armoury first and get a weapon, but I don't want just any weapon. I want my gun. I know my gun will be in evidence. When I get to the evidence door, my stomach sinks. It is electronically locked. You need a key card to get in. Of course you need a fucking key card to get in. This is a police station. I try to open the door regardless and it doesn't budge. It would take me forever to break in, if I could break in at all. I need to find a key card.

Back to the elevator I go. I press the button. This time, as expected, the elevator is here. It hasn't gone anywhere. When the doors open the eyeless officer greets me. I lean down and search him. I find hand cuffs, car keys, pack of gum, one small blue lighter, pack of cigarettes (I smile), key card (bingo), and his wallet (which I leave). I stand pocketing everything except the cigarettes, lighter, and key card, which I keep in my hand, and I strut back to the evidence door. I hear the elevator doors close when I get to the evidence door. I open the pack of cigarettes and light one. My eyes close reflexively as I suck down a large amount of thick smoke. Before I exhale, I slide the key card through the small magnetic slit. One single shrill beep followed by a red light. I exhale. No. This isn't happening. I do it again. Beep, annoying sound, red light. I go to do it again, but I freeze. *If you do that again this door won't open without a technician.* My hand shakes. I can't move my hand down. I'm watching, as I'm no longer steering my body. *Allow me.* I don't fight. I leave the card between the slit, and it stays. I go to a small box under it and snap it open. A small circuit board waits. I cross wires but don't understand why or what I'm doing, or I should say not doing. The light goes green, and the door unlocks. This time, I rescue the card, knowing I should and controlling my body. What the hell, I ask, in my head like someone will answer. They don't.

I walk into the evidence room, which is more like an evidence warehouse. When I see the size of this room, I almost get sick. How the fuck am I going to find my stuff? My eyes flick around, absorbing the room's entirety. I look for repetition and signs of order, some key in helping me cut down my search. The more time I spend analyzing the more guided I feel. I don't know this room, but I feel like I'm starting to. I walk in, almost drawn to one area, even when I can't be. I do start to understand the filing system. Dates, initials, acronyms seem to all jump out at me as I walk. Somehow, I compile them quickly and concisely. I'm learning. I don't know how but I am. If I wasn't so involved in the order of this room, I'd notice all the drugs and money that litter the shelves, packed neatly away, kept chronologically by the dust that builds on them. I see a box, under the box on the shelf a ticket hangs, and on the ticket are initials: J.R.V. Smudged on in sharpie and under them a date. Those are my initials and the date I was brought in originally. Before my rescue. I lift the box off and place it at my feet. I drop the cigarette I barely smoked and butt it out. I cut the seal on the box with my thumb nail and open it.

I walk with the open box toward the evidence clerk's desk. Which is now just a desk because the evidence clerk isn't here, and he or she isn't coming back? I place the box on the desk and sit down in the clerk's chair. I know what is about to happen. I know I don't want what is about to come but I need my gun. So, in a deep breath, I spill the contents of the box on the table. What I came home with spills out, neatly packaged in evidence bags, labeled cleanly. Despite the warning to not open, I tear the first one open wide, pulling one somewhat clean dress shirt out. Not the same dress shirt I was wearing, the one I obsessed about. Not the dress shirt that she sold me. This dress shirt is the one I was wearing when I rescued her from Sketch. The one Hane now has. This dress shirt covered in holes from the bullets he put into me as I watched him burn. I lay it out on the table. Another bag and I have the pants I was wearing. Another bag and I have my melted Zippo that I used to kill him. I put it on the table. I take my shirt off, my shirt that is covered in her blood. I almost forgot that I was still wearing the clothes she bled out on. I sit here, shirtless, empty. I let it happen because I know it will eventually, and I might as well get it over with.

I cry; I feel the salt run down my face. I feel it seep into my mouth, and I taste it welcomingly. I push my hand into my face and squeeze my eyes. I start sobbing. She's gone and I know this, I let this keep. I'll bury her soon. If it is the last thing I do, I'll bury her. I grab the bag that holds my gun, and I free it. I cycle it and check to see if it's functional. It is. Empty like me. Functional and empty like me.

I sit up, sucking in confidence, lighting a cigarette. I scratch my head with my empty gun and stand. I find the bag that has my holster and put my M1911A1 in it. I throw on my bullet ridden dress shirt and throw on my holster. I look at the black dress pants I've freed from evidence, and I look to my once white denim jeans that are now acid washed with crimson. I place the black dress pants back in the box. I'm keeping my jeans on. I don't tuck in my shirt. I just put my finger through one of the holes and find one of my bullet wounds that is almost healed. I sigh as I go through the remaining bags. I find my phone. I pocket that. I pocket my destroyed Zippo as well, just to remind me that Sketch is dead. I think I'm done here. I throw all the empty bags into the box to keep the one remaining piece of evidence – my black dress pants – company.

I take the box back to its place on the shelf and when I put it back, I see another ticket, with the same date, and my initials. I lift the small box off the shelf and tear it open. The only thing in this box is a tiny bag. In the tiny bag is a glass heart. This is all that they recovered and kept of Sketch, Becky's glass heart. I remove it and place it in the palm of my hand. I'm amazed and sick simultaneously. How did this heart survive the fire?

It did. That is all you need to know. Keep it. Remember that you still have a heart because I didn't.

I thought I got my life back. I remember everything. I remember you. Greyor. When I close my hand over that heart, I get something back I've been blocking, I get the knowledge that who I was, is who I am, but he is just more capable and I'm just reckless and lucky. I became him and he became me.

We are Johnny Valentyne.

I'm starting to sound insane, but this is my reality. One mind, split into two, living in one body. I remember more than grey or all black. I remember everything, though I don't want to. I need to pay attention. I need to bury her. I need to get out of here. I need ammo for my gun.

I close my eyes and suck down that sweet smoke and blow it out blindly. I leave the evidence room. I leave the evidence room with a slight comfort that I've retrieved the only things connecting me to a murder I would've gone to jail for. I'm now slightly washed of evidence that could convict me if this city or any city ever recovers from what is happening. Again, one piece of knowledge I'm without, and one I need to know.

I walk down the hallway toward the armoury. I have my bullet ridden white dress shirt on. I roll the sleeves up to my forearms exposing my assaulted wrists. I have my bloodied denim jeans sticking out of my untied black steel toes. I've got my gun and my holster with empty and awaiting clips. I think about what I'd look like to someone if all of this wasn't going on and I find humour that I fit in nicely because of this situation. I do everything to not focus on Greyor and the pain of losing Jess. I do it well because I've used that little trick and I'm now in the armoury with my jaw wide and my eyes peeled.

Guns, guns, guns. Countless, possibly every small machinegun to fully automatic assault rifles line each wall neatly. Enough fire power to start a war. Tactical gear, folding batons, flash grenades, and smoke grenades hang or sit placed perfectly in order. The first thing I grab is a tactical Kevlar vest. I remove my holster and take my empty clips. I toss it. I throw on the black Kevlar vest and close it. I grab a belt holster, putting my M1911A1 in it. I grab two folding batons, asps, and holster them. I grab some smoke grenades, two, holster them. I do the same for the flash grenades. I grab two frag grenades and throw those into pouches on the vest. I'm heavier but still very mobile. I go to the ammunition and pull out two boxes of .45 ACP. I load my gun and three extra clips. I fill my belt with all the .45 ammo it can take. I grab a HK USP .45, load it, and holster that on another belt. I grab an assault shotgun and load that, equipping the belt with all the shells it can take. I sling it over my shoulder. Ok, I'm ready for war, my own war.

I leave the room and sabotage the door so it can't be opened. I pull out a cigarette and light it. When I turn back to the hallway to leave a woman clad in similar gear greets me. She has a shotgun pointed at my head, and she fires. I feel pain and it goes black. I think I'm dead.

THE BEGINNINGS OF A BAD THING

I'm pulled down a hallway, not any hallway but one of many that infest Southstone. *I'm not dead, I'm unconscious, good, I think. This could be hell.*

I'm younger, much younger, probably within the first year of my imprisonment. I'm severely beaten, and I'm being dragged toward the courtyard. Two retrievers pull me through the doors and toss me into the courtyard. I hit the cold ground and suck in air. I wipe the mass of blood that blinds my vision. I look up and I'm greeted by Sketch.

"How many times are you going to do this to yourself?" Sketch asks.

"As many times as, it takes to me to get out of here. I am not who you say I am. I shouldn't be here. Let me go!" I scream between bloody teeth.

He kicks me hard in the mouth and I topple backward. Fresh blood runs freely and new pain sears with it, forcing me to remain conscious, and allowing me the strength to retaliate.

"Well, if you aren't who we say you're, who the fuck are you then?" Sketch screams at me as he runs in and kicks me in the side, adding injury to my injury.

"Johnny…" I cough, tumbling through the mud.

"Sorry? What was that?" Sketch screams as he lifts me from the ground and pulls me to his face so I can smell his hot terrible breath.

"My name is Johnny…Johnny Valentyne." I spit blood and begin to stand turning toward him, I lunge at him, and just before I get to him, he pulls out his Glock and shoots me in the chest, point blank range, intending the bullet fired to find my heart, sever ventricles, and pass through me; burying itself in the cold ground below. It does everything intended. He releases me, and as he does, he holsters his weapon by spinning it on a finger, flipping it so it points in the right direction, and then finally returns it from where he just drew it, like a cowboy after a gunfight.

"Well, he's dead, and now you're too." Sketch says trying to salt his rage.

As I fall, everything slows, and speeds up again when I hit the ground. I feel blood fill my lungs. I cough but they just fill. I feel myself drowning in my blood. I go still. Before I leave this, I hear a voice, a familiar voice, not to me then, but I know it well and I want to cut it off.

"Sketch what the fuck are you doing?" Silk screams storming out the double doors. He doesn't look how I remember him looking. His face is different. His face isn't like mine.

Sketch shrugs, looking away like a guilty child, but this isn't a joke to Sketch. His face can't hide the fear that melts away his rage. He knows he shouldn't have done that. I've never—or let me say I don't remember ever—seeing Sketch like this – or should I say like that.

"If he dies. You're dead." Silk says and Sketch stays quiet.

"Get him to Hanson, now." Silk screams at the retrievers. They run to lift me and carry me out. I watch Silk walk toward Sketch who folds back fearfully. Silk reaches out to touch him and his face twists in horror, like a recoiling animal knowing instinctively it is about to die. Silk stops just before touching him and smiles.

"I won't, I should, but I won't. Come on. Let's go see who's right about him."

I'm on a gurney and Hanson desperately tries to restart my heart, he continues to throw the paddles down and releasing current into my chest. My body responds but my heart doesn't. He has already used the maximum allowable current. Any more and my heart will explode. He's got the bullet out, but I've lost too much blood. According to science you can lose up to forty percent of your blood without dying, here, I've lost far more. The ringing beep that should be a thumping heart beat turned mechanical rhyme on the monitor screams in the silence of the room and Sketch hangs his head, as I remain, flat lined. Silk, furious and annoyed, turns to Sketch and walks toward him.

"Silk, come on, he wasn't going to work anyways. He can't be controlled. He is too much trouble and would bring too much attention if he had one of those relapses in public." Sketch protests, walking backward, looking for the door.

"No, he wouldn't, because the only ones who would remember him are the ones he was going to kill. Now, he's dead, and you my friend will follow." Silk says, walking with his arms out like he intends to hug Sketch.

"Are you off Silk? People would see us...remember us dragging him off and shocking him. No one in their right mind would turn away. Someone would see it and someone would report it. We would be up shit creek without toilet paper to clean our paddles." Sketch says, pulling at his ponytail, backing into two retrievers that stop him.

"Let me the fuck go." Sketch yells.

"Nice reference Sketch, but you're still wrong, we spent too much time and as I said, the only ones who can see us or remember us are being eliminated. The drug Sketch, the drug has been released already, has continued to be released…"

"What? How? What're you doing? Releasing it in the water?" Sketch fires back, cutting Silk off, still fighting to free himself from the retrievers.

"We have released parts of the drug. In the water supply; in headache medication, in birth control, in anti-histamines, in anti-depressants, antipsychotics, mood-stabilizers, and vitamin pills, in drugs; any chemical compound that enters into the city for the last several years has had a chunk of our drug in it, hidden away, waiting. Life stands still when we want it to and those who aren't affected, we kill. The insurance money just grows. The company renews it. Make sense now? The insurance is just a small part Sketch, just like you, unimportant in the big pretty picture." Silk smiles, cleanly, finishing his sentence and he now stands just in front of Sketch. He lifts his hands and goes to touch Sketch. What happens next causes a small segment of myself to die knowing that I prolonged Sketch's life.

One single beep rings loudly in the room in the absolute silence, cutting clean through it, stopping all action and bringing all attention to me. That beep is followed by another and then another. Silk turns, widely smiling, and he begins to clap as the monitor—despite the impossibility of it—goes from the single tone that is Asystole (flat line) to palpating murmur as my heart beats. Sketch sighs uncontrollably, eyes wide, and walks freely. Silk turns slightly but doesn't look at Sketch.

"I told you. Try and try and try but this Johnny boy just doesn't know how to die. We need him. I want him, alive, and functioning, for us, understand?" Silk states so sternly that it gets his message across and somehow everyone in the room knows not to answer.

WE SHOULD REALLY RUN, RUN JOHNNY, RUN

I open my eyes to more pain, but it isn't past pain, it is now, attacking my skull and swelling a goose egg lump at my hairline. I've been shot and knocked unconscious with a beanbag fired from a shotgun. It could be worse, could've been a slug, but if it was, I'd be dead. That rushing pain to my skull is followed by more pain, the pain of metal cuffs tightly cutting into my already wounded wrists that are held firmly behind me.

"You gotta be fucking kidding." I spit out slowly and groggily.

"Who are you?" The female officer questions with her shotgun placed at my balls.

I look down and then look up. It could be worse, I could be dead, but seriously, that barrel has to move and that is the only thing I care about right now.

"Can you please aim that elsewhere, hell, at my head if it makes you comfortable, because it would definitely make me compliant because I can't focus if you leave that there." I look up, trying to smile and focus on her as blood blocks my left eye.

She moves the shotgun and pokes my skull.

"Who are you?"

"Johnny."

"Johnny what?"

"Lady, honestly, does that really fucking matter?"

"It does, now, tell me who you are."

"Johnny Valentyne, my name is Johnny Valentyne. Now does that actually help?"

She doesn't relax the shotgun, instead, her posture gets rigid, and she tightens her grip on the shotgun that now sits on my forehead.

"Since we're doing introductions, what's your name?"

"My name is Kaitlin and I'm placing you under arrest."

"Are you out of your mind?" I try and stand from the wall, but she pushes the shotgun down harder on my wound.

"Lady, listen, we have to get out of here now." I scream, yielding, but asserting my sincerity for the need to escape despite being exactly where I was rendered unconscious.

"We're safer here than anywhere else." She says, looking down toward the elevator.

"No, no we're not, actually this is the..." I'm cut off by a seemingly small vibration. It grows and as it does, she gives notices. It gets stronger and stronger with every second that passes.

"What is that?"

"That is why we should get the fuck out of here."

"What is it? And how do you know what it is?"

"I can't explain right now, and even if I told you how I know, you wouldn't believe me if I told you, and because of this, we are already wasting time that we could be using to get us as far away from what is coming." I try and stand again but she forces the shotgun on me.

"How do you know what's going on?"

"Uncuff me and I'll explain while we're running away."

"No, get up, and explain everything now." She takes the shotgun off me and backs up, letting me rise, but still keeping her aim on my skull.

I stand, sliding with my back on the wall. I shake my head in protest and shrug. She points the gun from me to the elevator and then back to me. I stumble toward the elevator at her request. That vibration is now a sound. That sound is the sound of a thousand or more feet hitting asphalt and they get louder and louder, closer and closer. I look back at Kaitlin giving her a look of "I told you so" and I turn and stop at the mouth of the closed elevator.

"You need to let me go."

"I don't need to do anything."

She forces the shotgun into the small of my back and reaches past me and pushes that little button. A red light is followed by the sound of the elevator coming, and it distracts us both temporarily from the outside sound, and how much louder it gets by the second as what makes it gets closer and closer. The elevator arrives and opens, and as it does, I try to step back to stay here but she forces me with the barrel to get in and I don't argue. When we're in, she presses the ground button, and watches the doors close and when they do, she gives me her full attention.

"What's really going on?"

"Well, darling, that sound is bad. That sound is what a whole bunch of people coming here to kill us, or worse, rape, and then kill us, sounds like." I smile and attempt to turn my bound hands toward her, expecting and insinuating for her to release me. She isn't convinced, or amused, or compliant. She instead throws me into the closed doors of the elevator.

"Okay smart guy, if that's actually true, how do you actually know that if you've been trapped here?"

"Well, not like it matters, but I saw this in a dream. Or at least I think it was a dream, but I know it is coming...he wants me to know...to watch..." I recognize the insanity of my words, but I know I'm accurate, so I keep confident in the release of my sentence.

"A dream? A premonition? Ok Nostradamus, you're going out first." She laughs as she pushes the shotgun into me.

"Think about it. You've seen all the shit out there. Why would I lie, why would I make it up?"

"Because you're in cuffs now. Because you want out, and if you had a shred of sanity left, you'd know how many laws you broke and if you're convicted, sorry, when you are, you're fucked. Because I know, if I were you, I'd say anything to get free. But I'm not you but I know who you are and what you've done. So, you're under arrest, awaiting fair trial, and I'm going to make sure you get what is coming to you even if I have to walk you out of the quarantine. You heard the broadcast, this place is going to be a wasteland, and I intend to get out of here before it goes. I will bring you back with me even if I have to kill you and drag your body because you are paying for what you did."

"Get in line."

"What?"

"Get in line. I can't count the number of people who want me locked up or have tried. I can't list how many people have tried to kill me, want to kill me, or will continue to try. Lady, I'm involved in this; what's happening out there, and I intend to end it here. Nothing you do, and nothing anyone else does, will stop me from finishing what I started. Believe it or not but I wouldn't mind being arrested at this point, but I have to finish this so...even though I know what is waiting for me out there is terrible and seems undefeatable, I'm staying. I can't explain and honestly, I don't need to. I'll get out of these cuffs and fight my way out while you're being ripped apart out there." I finish evacuating my case and inhale, just as the elevator door opens. I turn to her, a smug look plastering my face; proud and positive, even in cuffs that painfully reopen the wound that just started healing.

We walk into the decimated hall. She's behind me, forcing me with the shotgun stuffed under my vest, pressed firmly against the small of my back. She leads me out toward the front of the building. The first thing I'm greeted by is silence; complete quiet. The absolute absence of sound, mechanical or natural are the first thing I notice. I'm offset by it. Shaken and hesitant, I walk toward—actually, no, the very ignorant officer forces me toward—the gap. This gap is what's left of the front doors to the police station. I try to slow. I resist the barrel momentarily but quickly yield to it because I know what it can due, or will, if I give the person wielding it a reason to cut me down. Never argue with someone who has a shotgun pointed at you at point blank range. I want to take in the surroundings, but she doesn't care. Unconcerned she forces me further. I know what's waiting beyond the blinding light of day. The light I haven't seen in a week or longer. My eyes still can't adjust. The natural light, foreign, now rapes my retinas entirely. I try and shield my face by turning into my body. Sadly, ineffective, because I tumble into the light and without my hands, I'm overwhelmed, catching my balance, stumbling.

My eyes adjust rapidly, retinas flaring; captivated completely by the natural light, and as they adjust granting me vision, the absolute unnatural sight that stands before me. People in the hundreds; maybe thousands; possibly tens of thousands surround the building, patiently waiting; like a crowd behind a barrier watching a parade. They don't seem concerned about me stumbling out. They don't notice. No one reacts. Not a single person moves. They all are frozen. As far as I can see, they remain perfectly still, completely absent of anything. They could be mall mannequins if they wanted to, but I doubt that a single one of them chooses to be like they are. Statuesquely, they peer on, somewhere beyond this building, beyond me, and beyond her.

I want to turn and look to what they are looking at, but I know they aren't looking at anything. Somehow each and every single person stands still, gazing aimlessly, absolutely comatose. Then suddenly, they part as if told to, but no voice and no sound signals them. They do. From within the sea of unconnected strangers one man calmly walks out.

I stand up. Pulling my eyes open and fighting the brightness. I force myself to focus and see. Forcing my attention, and bear witness to what is happening even though this can't be real, it very much is. I blink painfully through my past state, batting away the blind from my eyes. I see him, finally, and I see him now physically for the first time, not in a dream, and not in a memory. I know him and I don't all in the same moment. With my front toward him, every last particle of me screams his identity and it spells it out with only one word: enemy. I roll my shoulders and stand up straight to prove I'm ready; trying to convince this man that I'm ready for anything he throws at me, even though we both know I'm not. I'm visibly bound. I'm a prisoner. My hands are fixed behind my back. Surrealistically, I look around. I want this to be as fictional as it feels. I want this to me another false memory. I want this to be a nightmare, and I know with undeniable certainty it isn't when he speaks.

"What does it feel like?"

His voice comes from everywhere all at once. It cuts in and I hear every word leave his breath. I'm overwhelmed by the sound of everyone here speaking what he speaks. Not repeating but following every word like they've heard it before, as though they've practiced this moment over and over again. I know this shouldn't feel real; shouldn't be real, but it is.

Kaitlin reminds me of the control she thinks she has. The cold barrel slides under my vest as she lifts my shirt and forces it into the base of my spine. She is terrified but hides it well. She is obviously questioning everything but remains adamant and tries to rationalize why she is still here and the point of it all, as she forces me forward.

"Get out of the way. Return to your homes. I have no information for you other than it isn't safe to be away from your homes."

Asserting order, trying to find a place to ram it between the chaos that was and whatever this now is.

"Kaitlin?" The man calls with his many voices while we slowly walk on in front of the affected that watch us only with their eyes, and just their eyes, all at once. Once we are away from one set of pupils, too far from the peripheral, countless other eyes quickly replace the previous, burning a hole in us.

"Ignore him." I say, even though I know she can't, I bark at her without turning around, as she pushes me down the sidewalk.

"Kaitlin?" The man. The man I know as Ian Hane calls out to her. Every time he speaks, they speak. He talks through them and the sound is deafening and absolutely impossible to ignore.

"Do you remember what Ryan did to you behind the shed near the apartment you grew up in? Do you remember what you felt like after he was finished?"

She stops but I don't. I walk on like that barrel is still dug in my back; forced forward. I get three steps away and I can't move any further. I can't leave her to this. She doesn't know what comes next and neither do I, but I have some dark idea of what it will be. Her barrel slowly scans the crowd for his voice. She searches for his impossible voice and its beginnings. When she passes him the first time, I'm by her side, and I feel her trembling. When the barrel quickly snaps back returning to where it should be and realizing who is talking, I'm whispering in her ear.

"Uncuff me."

She lifts the shotgun and takes aim.

"Uncuff me right fucking now."

Her finger glides, sliding down, and stopping over the trigger.

"Uncuff me. You need to uncuff me. Uncuff me now!"

When the beanbag leaves the chamber, I jump up, I'm in the air, pulling my wrists down and under my bending knees, and then in front of my arching legs, pulling them up toward my waist. As the round passes through the unflinching crowd toward its target, deep within the crowd, a fraction of them suddenly come alive. They change from their statuesque, linear, solidity into fluent and collapsing defensive wall, protecting the intended target completely. One of the many that moved topples over from impact of the beanbag round. More move out of order and begin to charge us. Some move to block her last target. Several stand in the path of the last round, completely hiding Hane. The round only takes that one down as a sea of people flood forward, synchronously, taking off from an invisible starting line.

That first round beckons them, beginning the race as they sprint and sprawl forward toward the finishing line, us. I hit the ground with my hands in front of my chest; in the same moment they reach her. Within her gauge, I tug at her key chain and feed a single key into the first lock on the cuff I find. When she fires a second time, I'm inside the second lock. When those round hits another and as she goes to gauge again, stepping backward, the cuffs fall and I'm retreating backward, drawing my gun.

She disappears into the mass as they pile over her. Fighting each other to get at her first. I draw back the hammer and take aim. My finger squeezes out an entire clip, removing seven people from her, but I still can't see her. I don't reload. I holster my gun and rip the asp out of my belt and in one fluent—blink of an eye— motion it becomes a bat. I step forward, clipping the first to reach me, hard across the jaw, dropping him. The people swarm around us. I fight to stay free. I can't see her, but I can hear her. She screams for help.

She shrieks, gutturally, it is pure sound that contains no language. Her shrieks are cut off suddenly and replaced by gags. Something restricts her from screaming but allows just enough air. I furiously cut down everyone who comes at me, but I'm quickly overwhelmed. As hands and bodies take me downward, the asp is gone, and now I fight just to stay standing. With my only free hand I go into my tactical vest as I'm pulled downward. I bring a single grenade to my mouth, tearing the pin, and I toss it blindly. Arms and faces cut out the sky above like crossing your fingers and collapsing your hands over your eyes. I watch the grenade fly away. I feel the pummelling and kicking. I can only see flesh as I try and fight. The sky is gone.

I don't hear the grenade go off. I feel it. Then sound, nothing but the continuous ringing in my ears as I'm thrown concussively backward with a dozen people. I see the fire momentarily but a blanket of red and flesh replaces it. Crimson warmth paints me as I hit the wall of the police station that was far from me before the blast. I feel warm chunks slide down my face and arms, some small, and some large. I can't hear. The ring cuts out the sound. I'm free and unharmed but I'm soaked in the gore of countless people. I stand, wavering, but aware. I look to the mass and a chunk has been cut out of it. Bodies litter the ground from half way into the mass. I can clearly see Hane. The grenade went off and opened a gap in the crowd large enough to see exits. Some recover from the explosion. Some of them are solid and some of them don't realize they're going to die. I look for the cop. She too was shielded but I'm unsure of her condition. I try and run forward but fall several times, partly due to the disorientation, and partly because I trip over the dead.

Hane stands untouched and amused; a disturbing smile that almost consumes the entirety of his face shakes me. His head tilts slightly as though he tries to clear water from it. He watches but doesn't react. As I move over the dead, I pull my gun and reload it. I slide up next to her, tearing from the prison of bodies. Her vest is gone, and her clothes are torn and hanging. The explosion didn't hurt her, but the crowd mauled her. Her face is swollen and she's unconscious and nearly naked. The crowd watches with Hane, changing their posture, moving backward, allowing me space.

I holster my gun hesitantly and lift her. I look at Hane, whose eyes burn into me. The crowd steps forward, but only by one step. I back up, looking for my out. The silence is sickening as is the anticipation of his next move. I move as though I'm trying not to anger an already pissed animal. I glance quickly to the building next to the police station, he glances there too, and so does his army.

When I move toward it, they take another step, following my pace perfectly. I feel that shock of surprise and the sweat that follows it when Kaitlin shudders, jerking to consciousness, scrambling for breath, and crying out loudly in pain.

"Can you walk?"

She cries, cradling into me, struggling to accept her situation.

"I..I.."

"Can. You. Walk?"

She looks up at me, swollen, bloodied, and through nearly shut, puffy, and watering eyes goes to speak, chocking on the mess of her mouth.

"Yes. I'll try."

I help her stand. Her legs shake painfully. In shock she tries to cover her one exposed tit as though it is important that it isn't seen. I keep my eyes on Hane. Beside him, one of the affected has the shotgun I took from the police station. Near that guy, a woman has my asp.

"I know you're in pain, but I need you to move, ok?"

She nods.

We slowly back up, and as we do the crowd creeps forward, following us, and leaving Hane watching.

"I know what you want Johnny, and it isn't that way."

Hane and the crowd call out to me.

Shoot him Johnny, shoot him now.

"Valentyne. You let me out. Now let's have..." They speak again.

All in the same moment: Kaitlin reactively pulls from my assistance, confused, and hatefully stares at me like what happened to her is my fault—which it is—but indirectly. I can't hear the rest of Hane's sentence because it is interrupted by the revving of a very powerful engine, quickly followed by the thudding slap of people being run over, and immediately after that, the sound of the engine is drown out by heavy assault rifle rounds that cut around me. I move without thought, trying to pull Kaitlin with me. She is thrown backward, torn to shreds, and pulled from my grasp by armour piercing rounds. I don't try and rescue her because she is dead before her fingers fly free and limply release me. I move across a parking lot as bullets liquefy solids. People and cars literally melt, as what I can only guess is tungsten carbide obliterates them. Surprisingly, some affected rush to shield my escape, or at least it looks that way. I glance back, Hane is gone, and a once white, now red, Chrysler three hundred mows down people, chasing me. From the passenger window, one of the twins hangs out, unloading a large assault rifle, trying to end me.

I feel concrete explode, raining down over me, as I run into a parking garage of all things becoming one of my many bad decisions. In a running slide I duck under the yellow pay bar and pounce to my feet, veering right, and then diving behind a row of cars as the Chrysler breaks through and slides to follow me. I do my best to run, keeping my head down, as the trigger-happy twin just picks cars at random and fills them with rounds.

I hear the click, the beautiful symphonic ring of empty cartridge. I run faster than I thought possible and leap between a gap catching the second level barrier and pull myself over it. I hear the rev as they drive toward the second level. I'm on my feet and moving between rows of cars, heading toward the third level. I hear the sound of his gun as I dive down and feel glass and metal fly free. The violent echo of his assault rifle is deafening as I crawl, watching the wheels of their car bounce as they land and turn after me. I consider retaliating or rather I burn to, but I know that my vest will do sweet fuck all against an assault rifle, especially one with rounds like that. My only choice is avoidance and forcing him out of ammo. Not wise, because I don't know how much he has, but I don't have a choice. Praying for the sound of a different calibre isn't a plan but it's what I got. I go into my vest for the flash bang; I pull the pin and toss it over the car I'm behind.

The magnesium burns off with a loud bang and a hot flash and they smash into a nearby car. I run from my hiding place, digging out a smoke grenade, dropping it behind me as I sprint for the third and final level. Thick opaque smoke spins out, filling the second level, screening and covering my escape.

I reach the third level and sprint toward the barrier. I can see the roof of a building that is slightly lower than the garage but in no way is it easy to jump too. I run faster. My lungs feel like they're about to pop. The sound of an engine forces me forward, harder. I push hard from the ground, seconds away from the barrier, I can feel the car close behind and I hear the rounds zip by. With one last strong push, I leap from the barrier, throwing myself across the void blindly.

I feel the car hit the barrier, while I'm still in the air. Shattered headlight glass follows right behind me. The building rushes toward me as I reach out to grab the ledge. I'm not going to make it. Everything goes black and I suddenly and frighteningly lose consciousness.

ALLIES IN ALLEYS

"We take the transit-way. It's the best option. We're home free when we get to the depot. Will steal a bus and ride it out on the highway and get as far as we can from here." Max spits catching his breath.

Thirteen people huddle, crouching: keeping themselves out of sight. They've made it across the city using transit stations and transit-ways and have stopped to catch their breath and regain some energy before having to cross what could be a very populated area to get to the destination their appointed leader chose.

"Max, what about Johnny?" Manny takes his time finishing his sentence nearly passing out when my name flies through his lips.

"He'll be ok."

"How do you know?" Salina says, shaking Manny, helping him hold his head up.

"Who's Johnny?" Laflamme asks.

"Our friend." Everyone, with the exclusion of Zachary and Sarah answer synchronously.

"How do you know he isn't like the rest of them?" Laflamme questions as innocently as possible.

Zachary looks at Sarah and goes to speak but stops himself as Max clears the silence.

"He isn't."

"Yeah, but how do you know?" Laflamme disregards sincerity.

"He is immune to what caused this." Manny pipes back up.

"What caused this?" Jen asks.

"Drugs." Max sighs.

"Drugs?" Tanner asks.

"Listen, we don't have time for this. We have to keep moving." Brand points out what everyone knows but isn't able to accept.

Shawn all the while looks back down the tunnel, down the way they came. Tristan sits against the wall spinning his gun. Salina and Aila help Manny stand. Zachary and Sarah help them. Jen and Tanner follow. They begin to slowly move forward toward a descending staircase that will take them back into a concrete jungle full of enemies and that jungle separates them from the depot.

"Pardon me, but I don't know any of you, and I trust you less than I know you...so, before I go any further with you, explain something...how is it that you all are not affected and know the same guy?"

Laflamme stops suddenly, smirks widely, almost like he knows the answer, as though he asks rhetorically.

Most of the group move forward while Laflamme and Max stay behind.

"I can't give you an answer. We don't know why..." Max looks up ahead, watching the group grow smaller in the distance.

"...We aren't all unaffected, Manny...Manny is sick..."

"You think he is becoming one of them, don't you?" Laflamme says, replacing his smirk with sincerity, or at least what sincerity is supposed to look like.

"...Yeah, Johnny told me something, something that didn't make sense, but it is starting too." Max says while sighing.

"And what's that?" Laflamme, again, asks a question that sounds far too rhetorical.

"Don't take any drugs. He said it several times. He called me from a police station the day everything went too shit. He didn't sound like Johnny; he sounded different somehow. He didn't ask me to bail him out or tell me what the fuck was going on. He just said don't take anything, didn't matter where from, bottled or street, just don't take anything." Max says, walking forward, signifying that they should catch up.

Laflamme nods, smiles, and then follows. While Max turns, Laflamme looks back down the tunnel. He is looking for something or someone, but Max doesn't see.

The rest of the group already on the other side of the second transit station stop to catch their breath, waiting for Max and Laflamme to catch up.

"Manny, hun, look at me." Salina shakes Manny's face, cradling his head in her hands.

Manny hangs between Zachary and Sarah's shoulders and Salina stands in front of him.

"Baby, please, look at me." Salina weeps because Manny can't lift his head or doesn't try.

Max and Laflamme come through the corridor and are out of earshot from the rest of the group.

"Why hasn't Manny become like everyone else?" Laflamme questions Max through his bouncing breath.

"He has a thyroid problem maybe that is why he hasn't changed into..." Max replies.

"But he will." Laflamme coldly replies, cutting Max off.

Max breaks and turns stopping Laflamme,

"Listen buddy, watch the next words that come out of your mouth. That is my best friend, and he just needs his pills." Max almost screams but controls his voice, so the others don't hear him.

"You don't know that. Listen, I'm sorry but you have to know this won't end well, now, or later. The longer you wait, the harder it'll be." Laflamme says, throwing the hair off his face, exposing his features.

Max, suddenly taken back, takes a double look, unable to tell if Laflamme is a woman or a man,

"That isn't a conversation we are going to..." Max replies, cut off by Laflamme's expression and distraction. Max feels and looks for what Laflamme felt and now looks for; the rumble of a crowd running in their direction. A vibration caused by trampling feet followed quickly by the sound of a hundred charging footsteps smacking pavement, immediately followed by echoed wailing from within a tunnel not far behind them.

"Run!" Max takes off followed by Laflamme just as a horde of people smash through the doors they just came from. Max and Laflamme sprint toward the rest of the group shouting for them to run.

Manny lifts his head, a sick image smears his face and sweat inks from his pores. He groggily looks at Salina who's tears now dry.

"We gotta go baby." Manny says as he takes a step away from Sarah and Zachary, walking on his own, and then running as he grabs Salina and takes off. The group rally behind them with Max and Laflamme catching up. The horde of affected are just on the group's heels, following close enough to touch them, as they sprint out of the terminal and on to the open streets closing on them fast.

Max turns and fires into the swarm. Blast after thunderous blast tears from his shotgun as he walks backward toppling rows of ravenous affected. Max stops walking backward as he hears the click on his shotgun. He turns and runs, nearly caught by the horde, he leaps over a nearby car and runs off down an empty alley losing sight from the rest of the group.

Laflamme sprints with uncanny quickness, gaining on the group, and leaving the affected far behind, unconcerned by the loss of Max because Laflamme doesn't even look back.

The group sprints across the congested streets that resemble a car graveyard, almost identical in appearance to that of a junkyard. They run toward the next bus station that calls plainly in the distance. Close enough to see but too far to reach. Their hurdling pursuers don't seem to tire and with every push and exhausting inhale to exhale the group loses distance while the affected recover it. Tristan spins, and unleashes round after round, picking some off but the ones that fall only slow the rest, hopeless. At this rate they won't reach the next terminal and will be swallowed by the horde that tries to overrun them. When the hammer snaps back cold Tristan tries to catch up to the group. He feels the hands of affected reach for him, but they miss, but only by a step, so close that one keeps a piece of his shirt as he tears free.

When Tristan hears the rev of an engine, it wakes him, and when he feels it cut the hands off the affected that grab at him, it feels as refreshing as cold rain on a scorching day. When the sound of metal crushing metal cuts as close as the hands of the affected on his back, he smiles. A semi truck cuts between the encroaching horde and the group, closing the road off. The truck smashes into several cars and stops. From the driver seat of the truck, Max leaps out, and joins Tristan running, chasing the group as the recovering affected fight and spill over the truck after them.

THEY CAME INTO THE WORLD TOGETHER AND LEAVE IT THE SAME

I wake, on my feet, running. You'll never know true confusion until you wake up running. You will never understand urgency until you wake up running and the first thing you hear is gunfire. You can't understand confusion and urgency until you blackout mid leap from a parking garage to the closest building just to flee people trying to add orifices to your body. To make matters much worse is that you were falling, and sure, you were not going to make the jump, sickened, and helpless. You fell toward the building you jumped to and right before you caught it—or as I remembered, missed it—you lose consciousness. Where the fuck am I?

I am sprinting down a surprisingly empty street with the twins still gunning after me like a double entendre, guns, and engine, firing fully. I move around the few abandoned cars that are nearby. They ram through the obstacles trying to run me down or fill me with bullets. I roll and dive between untouched vehicles and as soon as I do, that vehicle is touched, and destroyed, forced and fed with bullets meant for me.

Move. Johnny, move. Another car comes from its petrified and abandoned position, spinning toward me, almost taking me from my feet. I hit the sidewalk and leap over a fire hydrant just as it's torn from the ground with a geyser shortly following, then comes the glass, lots and lots of sharp little shards raining down from my right from a store window. Bullets open store windows like a riot walking down the street. Each window explodes right behind my shoulder as I can feel the grill of their car licking at my heels.

I veer left and take the street, over one car, and around another. Both cars pushed after me. Another empty clip sound isn't a blessing but a welcomed break. I move faster somehow, digging deeper, tearing for more air and energy. I can't feel any part of my body; it feels like fluid less like flesh.

I dive over a car and don't feel gravity's embrace as I slide over the roof, denting it. I don't feel the glass of the store window as their car ramming the one, I was on tosses me from the roof and right through it.

I barely get off the ground and run toward the back of this clothing store I'm now in, and familiarizing myself very quickly with, as they follow me in with their car. I hit the side door with so much force I take the door with me. I'm followed by loud and terrible burst fire cutting the frame I stood in a second ago, obliterating it.

I'm back on the street just to see their beat-up Chrysler pull from the window and turn toward my direction. The Chrysler is without headlights, the front crushed inward. It looks almost like a crooked white and silver smile, malevolent. I just hear the engine roar as they chase after me. The car seems as angry as they are. I look back once just before nearly spilling over a car barely making it over its frozen mass. I hit the other side and move faster than before, and with more urgency than ever. I know I can't run for much longer. My lungs can't compete, and my heart feels like one single beat. I feel like I'm going to collapse and that is not just a thought, I will shortly because unlike them and their car and guns, I'm out.

The twins are relentless and gaining on me. The obstacles I use barely slow them and their ravenous hunger to end me. I come to a crossroads but don't follow a street because they're no more cars ahead and the ones further down the street aren't reachable

for me, and they've destroyed all the ones behind with
bullets and bashing.

Instead, I take my back against a telephone poll
and turn as I hear one twin empty the last of his clip
near me. I pull my gun and open fire. I don't aim for
the twins. I aim at one belt that buckles the only
secured twin, the one steering. Within my fire, I see
the buckle leave, and in his panic, he accelerates; he
wants to crush me between fender and post. I snake
around to the other side of the pole and brace, closing
my eyes, and inhaling so deeply I nearly vomit from the
first full breath I have had the chance to take in what
feels like forever. The car folds around the pole as
though attempting to meld with it and I feel a
hurricane of debris pass by me with the force of the
car cracking the thick wooden pillar, but it does not
fall.

The twins slide in separate directions, tasting
asphalt, and tearing flesh. They each leave a red trail
after flying through a once solid windshield and Swiss
cheesing before hitting and sliding across the
unforgiving pavement. They eventually stop sliding,
but not before losing most of their skin, and they stop
nearly at the same point. I walk between them,
exhaling and drawing my other gun. I stand between

them and fire both guns simultaneously. A bullet tears through each of their skulls, cementing their passage to death, and solidifying my belief that they are, without a doubt, and any shadow resembling one, dead. Born in the same moment and died in another. Goodbye, you sick fucking abominations, please rot or burn wherever you end up.

I smile, and let my body catch up. I feel the confusion and let it be. I thankfully appreciate what could be the few seconds of rest I am getting right now and then holster my weapons, searching, and learning my location.

Where the fuck am I?

Broken record words and thoughts rebound off the empty regions I call a mind,

I collapse backward and fall between the dead twins. I inhale and exhale, deeply, and slowly. I watch the encroaching night as it rapes the day. I let the exhaustion take me in the worst possible place but I'm without choice, as fucking always.

THE CRY FOR HELP

Henry opens his eyes slowly, and carefully. He can't hear very much, let alone see very much. He doesn't know how long he has been unconscious or what is going on. Since he met the Silk that looks like that me that night, he remembers nothing else, and that was weeks ago. He does know he is in a moving vehicle surrounded by people. Yet another thing he doesn't know is who they are and where they're taking him. He recognizes Silk's voice but no one else. He goes to speak, to call to Silk, but is smothered by Silks screams.

"Just run them down."

He hears the engine rev, and he feels the vehicle speed up. When the first impact happens, he doesn't understand it. When the next several follow. He can hear the sound of hands hitting the side of the vehicle. He knows something horrible is happening when the sound of the vehicle hitting something or someone and the sound of hands against the vehicle, his stomach grows sick.

"Mr. Crisante, how many fucking people are going to get in the way?"

"Everyone affected, so about ninety percent of this cities fucking population."

"What do they want?"

"They want to fuck you, kill you, or do both."

"What?"

"You heard me. Now, just get us to our destination, ok?"

The vehicle speeds up even faster and the sounds of bodies being hit and crushed under the vehicle meld with the sound of acceleration and a sudden and very hard, sharp turn.

Henry's eyes focus as he lifts his head.

"Boss, the doctor is awake."

"Well, welcome back to the land of the somewhat living Henry."

"Silk, what...how long have I been...where are we?"

"We're going to Grim Associations central office, located in the pristine heart of the city. Sadly, traffic is unreal."

"What is going on?"

"No time for that. Mr. Kiryk, would you please get us into the parking garage, and then when we are in, shut it down and keep them away from the entrance. I want a way out. Have your other team lead them away from us."

Henry jumps in, trying to turn the conversation back so he can comprehend what is happening.

"Did you release the drug into the general public?"

"Yeah, we have for some time, we just activated it a lot sooner than we intended too." Silk calmly responds, not looking back from the passenger seat. Henry sits in the very back row of this armored SUV.

"Are you crazy?"

"No."

The vehicle picks up speed, as it cuts through a crowd of people that are brawling naked, writhing, and fornicating.

"What is happening? This is chaos. What is the point of this Silk?"

"We disappear, as planned."

"I didn't plan this."

"No, no you didn't, we did. You just make the drugs."

"Does Alexi know about this? She could not have agreed to this; been aware of this… "

"She's dead."

Henry goes quiet for a second because who he thought was in control of this madness is now dead and it appears that Silk has taken over. That thought alone scares Henry, and it should.

"What?" Henry coughs out.

The SUV corners again, this time even harder, throwing Henry into one of the heavily armed soldiers that box him in. It heads down a large open stretch of road leading to an underground parking lot under a spiraling steel tower, followed quickly by another SUV, and streets behind both vehicles, legions of disturbed and furious affected chase after them.

Both vehicles collect speed as they hit the ramp and descend toward an empty garage. They stop at a large steel grate that separates them from the inner garage. One solider climbs out and runs to the security desk and hits the door release. The garage grate churns as it erects into the structure and disappears. The vehicles began to roll in as shadows take the remaining light of the sun that fills the ramp and the entrance of the garage, the last light of the sun, stolen by the volleys of affected that spill down the ramp and charge the gate. The lonely solider hits the button again and the grate begins to return as he walks backward, panicked; he opens fire into the crowd and tries to push them back. However, the crowd continues at him, without expression, or concern of injury. Both vehicles, once inside, skid to a stop and soldiers spill out from them. They all open suppressing fire, trying to keep as many of the affected as they can, out. Silk hops out and screams for a part of the soldiers to follow and to bring Henry with them. Henry is now out of his bonds and falling out of the vehicle. He goes into his pocket and pulls his cell phone, dialing a number. The gunfire is deafening already, but because of the closed in garage, the acoustics make the gunfire painfully deafening. Henry barely hears the phone call go to voice mail.

"Valentyne... its Henry. Silk has the cure. If you're alive, I need your help. We can stop this. Please, if you hear this, I need your help. He has me at the city center building, please..."

Henry drops the phone as he is dragged by one of the soldiers, who pulls at his collar with one hand, dragging Henry backward, all while firing a handgun at several affected that run toward him.

"Doc, let's go fuck! Get on your feet. On your feet, now!"

The soldier puts two down that get far too close for comfort as Henry is now on his feet running alongside the soldier that came to his aid. Silk watches as the gate crashes down finally and keeps out the horde of affected that have caught up to him and his little army. The group of affected that got in are gunned down quickly in perfect succession. One of his soldiers, the one that didn't make it through the gate after opening, screams for help beyond the grate as he is beaten, and his clothes are torn off. He holds onto the grate, crying for help as they begin to overwhelm him. His cries become whimpers as his voice is stolen by flesh and pain. One of his friends walks towards the gate and unloads an entire clip of his assault rifle into him, securing his friends passage to peace from the torment he knew only moments ago, killing him, and the monsters who took him.

"Why the fuck are they doing this Mr. Crisante? Why don't they just kill each other?"

The soldier questions as he walks toward the elevator that awaits him and his team.

"They have regressed to animals. You can thank the doc for creating this vicious serum. They are now only instinct, driven by what they know, to procreate and dominate. Come, we need to get what we came for and get out of here as quickly as possible. If you really need an explanation, I'm sure I can when we are far from here and enjoying all the money nobody will ever know is missing." Silk charismatically cues, keeping the elevator waiting for one of his many soldiers, smiling that smile, that if you didn't know him, you would never know that behind it hides a monster, masked by beauty.

Back near the gate, the call on Henry's phone ends, as the elevator doors close. That message now waits for me to wake and when I hear, I am coming to show men what monsters really look like.

THE STRAGGLERS

Becca, Shawn's lover, far from dead but not unscathed, has spent the last several days recovering in a house she doesn't know but will never forget. When Max rescued Shawn, Shawn was convinced Becca was dead, when what had really happened could easily be considered worse, but she wasn't. Instead, she was beaten severely, raped in every possible orifice, and left for dead. However, in the rescue of Shawn, she herself had been rescued, and dragged away to safety. That was a little over two weeks ago and now she sleeps in a ball, watched by her rescuer, a small blonde girl named Janny. Janny found her, and risked herself to bring her to safety, barricading them away from the confused and enraged affected that roam the streets looking for challengers; those who they can dominate or kill.

Janny, a musician, who had missed the initial chaos due to her creative side, had the misfortune and sudden realization that the world had lost its mind in her absence. She had just gone out to buy a pack of cigarettes and she witnessed the horror of the attack on two unaware lovers. Luckily, she intervened and saved Becca. She has and still keeps constant watch as the poor girl recovers. To Janny, the world had always been this mad but never showed it. However, she knew this was more than just the sickness of humanity, this was something else and she had prepared herself for this long ago.

Becca painfully wakes, looking around, and trying to imagine that what she remembers, is not a memory, but rather is only a nightmare, prays that it is; even when she knows it too be real. Janny greets her with her beautiful little smile; that smile understands or at least tries to understand her pain. It relieves that pain, even though momentarily and incrementally. Her smile carries across a calmness and sincerity that cannot be mimicked. This is genuine and in that genuine gesture, she finds shelter. Becca ignores the reality and sits up,

"Where am I?"

With Becca's voice something outside stirs and before Janny can say anything, her sanctuary is shattered as her front door comes off and affected spill in to find them. They scream out and their voice cuts through the silent city and finds me.

I wake to it, and the incessant sound of my voicemail telling me I have a missed call, but I'm conscious when I hear the sound of their cries, and before either is scathed, I'm on my feet, and I become their rescue; I am their salvation.

Several affected flood the room, three men, and two women. Becca and Janny move down the hallway toward the washroom. Their involuntary screams brought on by someone kicking in Janny's door gave away their place in the apartment, but they move quickly enough to barricade themselves in the washroom. I move into the apartment building where I heard the screams. The direction is easy to follow because the city is a graveyard. The building is less like an apartment and more like a heritage house. At some point, people would call this four-floored structure warm and maybe even call it home, but now, nothing more than a place to hide. From the looks of it, as I cautiously climb the stairs, this place must have been abandoned for weeks. Those who got out did, and those who stayed, fell victim to the slaughter. Blood smears the walls from drag marks. Signs of struggle and painful ends mark this place. Broken barricades and makeshift weapons litter the halls. Somebody put up a fight. Sadly, that fight ended horribly with even more innocent lives lost.

I bound up these stairs to the top floor and follow into the recently removed barricade into an apartment where the noise emanates from. I unfold my baton, and when that asp snaps open, it brings a sudden and unsettling silence. The first expressionless affected bounds from the hallway near the bathroom, into the living room, and turns toward the front door, the one that I now occupy.

He leaps over the couch and charges me, but I don't hesitate. I move under him and strike upward as he folds over me. The asp catches him under the jaw, and he folds to the floor. Before he gets up, I crack down on the back of his skull, caving it in. A sick mess paints the floor as I turn, and I'm greeted by the other affected. Somehow, I'm without hesitation, even when I know these people don't know what they're doing. My remorse is removed. However, as I strike at them, and as they spill toward me over the large sectional grey couch that separates us, I'm filled with a foreign emotion, fear. I back step, wildly swiping. While I collapse one woman's jaw, and watch her teeth sprinkle like dice across a nearby table, and she folds grasping her broken mouth, one of the men throws the other woman back. It looks like he is trying to protect her; the way an animal protects its mate, primitively.

This ignites apology even when I cannot have any and because of that, I freeze up. The man, her protector, spears me across the room.

I land on my back hard enough to feel it but not hard enough to wind me. My asp flies out of my hand and spins off under a table. As he strikes down at me, the other woman who isn't cowering and toothless jumps in. I don't waste time as the urgency of how important it is that I do not get pinned takes over; I don't know what they'll do to me, but I have some horrible idea. I catch his arm and pull him downward as I swing my legs up wrapping them around his neck and that arm, he hit me with, and I roll, pinching him between my thighs. As he loses air, his strength follows, but I feel his teeth in my leg, and a kick to my side from the other woman, I let go of him. As she comes in for another kick that's aimed at my face, I grab her leg by the ankle and I roll with it, pulling her down. I rise while holding her leg, and I step on her, and pull, dislocating the joint raw. She sucks in air to scream but does not, instead she just groans in agony as though she is confused by the injury and how it limits her. The other man comes at me again but is now joined by the toothless female. I kick him back as she leaps on me, blood pouring onto me, blinding me. I stumble backward. She swings wildly, cutting across my face with her fists, and she locks her legs around my waist. He has already recovered and returned to join in assaulting me, pulling at us both, trying to get at me. This resembles animals trying to prove who is more superior by being the first to kill their prey, and their prey is me. I have entered their territory, and I am the threat. The affected have gone from aggressive mindless beasts, killing to prove superiority, to pack animals defending their mates. They strike at me, and I cannot protect myself. Blow after painful blow, I lose my balance. Between her fists and his hands around my throat, I am losing.

However, when I hear the shrill cry from a girl in the washroom, something washes over me. When that shrill cry becomes a hauntingly woeful plea for help, I find clarity. Finally, when I hear the painful begging from her for him to stop whatever horrible thing, he is about to do to her or is doing to her, I become action.

I throw my arms under the woman's, guarding her blows, and I drive the crown of my skull into her nose so hard that it feels like it should've cracked my skull open, however, it destroys her nose, collapsing her septum, spraying hot blood down the front of us, and she falls off me instantly unconscious, if not dead. I knock his hands off my throat by swinging my arms down like an ape crushing its competitor. I grab his Adams apple, and sweep his feet, leaping with him in the air, I land on him as hard as possible. Winded, he collapses under me. I grab the first object I can find, a crystal ashtray, and as the ash flies and cigarette butts rain down, I crush his face inward with it. The ash mixes with his blood, and it looks like his face is smeared in dark, viscous mud. He is dead without doubt and any shadow that would resemble it.

I ignore the other woman, because she can't stand to stop me, and I leap over the couch running for the washroom.

Becca kicks the last affected man in the back when he bursts through the door, but he swings and knocks her across the washroom. She hits the wall hard, cracking her head on the tub. Janny hits him square in the face with a haymaker and he turns back to look at her with that empty expression, hauntingly dead, but within it, it is somehow hungry. He throws her against the tub and spins her. She kicks at him and tries to push from the tub, but he is too strong and too dedicated. She cries out, *I hear this,* and she tries to drag herself away from him as he tears her pants down exposing her ass. He pulls her toward him as she squirms and shakes but he pushes her down harder with his hand firmly over the back of her neck as he tries to enter her violently, pushing down hard with his hips like an animal attempting to instinctually mate. She pleads with him. She begs him not to, but he can't hear her because there isn't a shred of humanity left in this man, just an instinct to dominate. She whimpers, as she bites down hard into her lip, and tears stream down her face anticipating the painful penetration and holding back the sickness of helplessness as she feels him so close and now the sharp pain as he forcefully tries to enter her.

The next thing she feels isn't the impaling entrance into to her but the force of him being torn off her by me. We land in the tub pulling down the shower curtain with us and he violently flails to get me off his back, but I don't wait, I wrap the shower curtain around his head and twist, wrapping my legs around his waist and I can unfortunately feel his hard prick flopping against my legs as he fights me. Janny crawls away from the tub, watching us struggle in the transparent curtain and she prays I kill him, but she also worries that I'm just as bad. She doesn't know who I am or where I came from, but she is glad I came before he got to.

He throws violent elbows into my vest in one last struggle to get me off, but each hit grows weaker and weaker by the second and luckily, my Kevlar vest helps pad the damage he tries to do to my ribs. He finally stops but I don't let the pressure up, I just lay there with this naked man, now monster, with a shower curtain attached to his face, catching my breath. Janny pulls her pants up, but she does not stand up, and because of that, she can't see beyond the mouth of the tub. She quietly crawls to Becca and tries to wake her.

She shakes Becca conscious but before Becca can make a peep, Janny roughly smothers her, stopping her from speaking. In the small recess of this tub, I violently regain my breath and composure. I know how scared they must be, and I know that they might be scared of me. Becca motions for Janny, signaling her silently that they need to escape right now. That is when I choose to sit up. Janny selflessly shields Becca. I release the brute from my dead man's grip, and he limply slides down in the tub, slowly screeching, as I roll him off me. Janny doesn't know if I'm friend or foe, but Becca does. I don't know how she does because not even Jess recognized me, but Becca does, her eyes calm and she begins to rise, speechlessly. Janny, on the other hand, does not.

"Get back, get the fuck back." She barks at me and tries to stop Becca from approaching me.

I walk from the tub, slowly, and quietly and as I do, I harmlessly raise my hands, completely defenseless. Becca has always had this strange ability to make anyone comfortable, at any time, just with her presence. She always calmed me down. It is utterly horrible that I lost my life and forgot people just like her, and now insanely liberating that they are not all gone even when I know how they have made it this far.

She pushes past Janny peacefully, and Janny complies, confused but now calm. Becca wraps her arms around me and squeezes me so hard I can't breathe.

"Johnny?"

"Yeah, Becca?"

"What took you so long?"

"I lost myself."

"And now?"

"Let's get you out of here..."

I say calmly. Before I speak another word, I focus on my subconscious and the track it follows like a train, and I attempt to understand the direction it takes...

Don't you find it extremely unsettling that so many people you know are still alive and mostly okay? I mean, I'm glad they're alive, but Johnny, this is the farthest thing from convenience, and you know it, and despite Silk confessing that he helped keep them alive and well; don't you feel as though this is all still wrong? Articulate as he may be, no one is perfect. Maybe this is a trap? Maybe your friends are Silk's contingency to keep you busy? Maybe, he knew. Maybe he knew that you are so stubborn and incapable of loss and that you would survive, escape, and pursue. He might have known this and because of his belief in your resilience, believed that death for you wasn't certain. Moreso, maybe, or actually, he was sure that you couldn't die; wouldn't die. Maybe he anticipated this, you trying to help others left over, and he now is betting that you will try and save the remainder of the life he let live and you left behind because he knows you. You have to consider and challenge everything now. Just like it was, like he said before you thought he was dead. Nothing is cement or solid, everything is fluent or transitory.

My mind, my former grey or all black mind, begins to attempt to make sense of things that may not make sense at all, but just in case they might, I try to. I just don't really know for certain and without doubt why my friends are all still alive; beyond Silk's supposed back up plan. Which, come to consider it, could be entirely bullshit, but more importantly, I know they are alive, and that is all that matters. Lies or no lies, I will save those who are alive and avenge those who aren't. As I ponder, I'm interrupted, as always, as chaos comes knocking, and completely cuts me off violently...

I would first like to explain what the most horrible sounds on the planet are, at least, for me. The world makes noises and so does its inhabitants. The absence of sound is terribly discomforting. Like something horrible is about to happen, or something truly malicious is on its way too harm you, and when it is, silence is terrifying. Now, the second most terrifying sound would have to be the sudden snapping of that silence. For instance, a gunshot, but not any gunshot, but for me it seems to be a gunshot while I occupy the small space of a washroom. Then the third most horrible sound is the ringing in your ears, the perforation of the eardrum, the absolute pain. Finally, the winner in the most horrible sound contest would have to be—*keep your fucking drum roll*—the return of sound and the realization of what, or who, just received the bullet that ended said silence.

I exhale silently; I am shocked, and terrified of who fired and who got hit. My eyes stare at a small blonde girl, Janny, who is frozen like me. The auburn-haired girl, Becca, still in my arms, holds me tighter, but does so with only one arm, because her other hand holds my smoking M1911A1, pointed at the man in the tub. Her pull trigger is surprisingly and electrically quick. She just wants to be sure he is dead.

I let my guard down and now everyone is coming for us. As I said, Becca has always had a way to make me feel comfortable, even in the worst situations. It could be worse, and it is about to get a lot worse, but these girls aren't dead, and as long as I'm still breathing, I'm going to keep them that way.

"Babe, give me my gun, we have to go…right now…" I look down at her and I smile, carrying a sincere yet false confidence that everything is going to be fine.

"I'm not going to let anything happen to you, either of you…"

I look at Janny and flash a warm smile, somehow, a new smile, and with my new smile, I extend my hand.

"I'm Johnny. And I'm going to get you out of here."

Becca slides the gun into my hand. I put the hammer down slowly and holster it. I walk out of the washroom with Janny and Becca following closely behind. I stop suddenly, retrieve my asp from under the table, and just absorb the world around me. More specifically the sound I focus on that doesn't belong to the washroom, or its pipes, or the building, and all of its various sounds. I'm trying to hear what is coming from outside the building, the sound that seeps in from a window in this hallway.

I look out as a sea of people charge toward the building and I'm left in awe. They come from snaking streets and spill from what I thought were empty buildings. An entire city coming after these girls, and me and if I could feel anything besides my heart pounding in my chest from my last fight, I'd feel the fear take hold. When it comes to flight or fight, in this case, I'm going with the later and I mean fucking fast. I turn only briefly, and speak one word that I don't need to, but the girls instantly listen,

"Run."

And we do. As if the most terrible thing chases us. And it does. We move out of the building and spill on to the street. We need something faster than feet. We need a vehicle. And I need Henry and answers. But these girls need to live unscathed and I'm going to make damn fucking sure they do.

I tell the girls with a point of my finger where to run, and I tell them I'm right behind them. I run toward the twin's annihilated vehicle and pull from the seat that beautiful assault rifle and I dig around the back of the car for ammo. When I find it, two clips of it, I don't waste time, I load it, and I run again.

"Where are we going?" Janny screams back at me.

"A dealership."

"Which one?"

"Doesn't matter but I don't know this area anymore, take me to the closest one, and fast."

Janny looks back and almost smiles, knowing that is the dumbest thing I've said since I've met her. She motions with a head jerk and turns and runs down a side street. And I realize, with that, I have a message on my phone. I draw my phone from my pocket and press one, letting it dial my voicemail while I load the assault rifle. Janny and Becca stop and turn to me.

"Are you fucking serious right now?" Janny screams at me. I greet her question with a finger that implies for her to keep quiet, and I'm surprised when she does.

"Your phone works? How?"

She questions again, which I ignore. Good question though: How does my phone still work? I can only assume our company phones work on a different frequency. It is the only explanation as to why Henry and I can make and receive calls. How can no one else use this frequency? Another good question, and I don't have an answer.

I listen to the voicemail and for the first time in a long time, I feel hope, despite everything. I don't care what happens to me but if I can fix this, or stop this, I have to try. I just have to get Alrick. As I finish listening to the message, a group runs from a street toward us. I stop, aim, and ready my new weapon. I bring the assault rifle up and take aim. As they fall and slide with every new slug I waste, I smile.

"We need a ride. Let's go."

I follow the girls and keep affected back as we head toward a car dealership. I have a plan, if you can call it a plan. I get Alrick, and then we get out of the city. As we run toward the dealership, I hear an explosion and see smoke, and I know what that is. It is a sign. A sign someone is still alive. Someone has just blown up a gas station and I bet my life it is my friends. Now I just have to get Alrick and these girls to my friends so they can all get out. I will make this happen. When I pocket my phone, I miss the notification that I have another voicemail waiting.

WHAT IS RIGHT AND WHO IS LEFT; DRAWING STRAWS

Max sits back gauging the last seven shells into his shotgun, and then he checks the hunting rifle he found minutes ago.

He looks around his friends, some new, and some old but one of them isn't a friend and Max knows it, this Laflamme character is up to something, but Max has had no time to deal with him or her, still unsure of his or her sex. Laflamme sits perched across the room staring out the window.

Max looks away from Laflamme briefly to check on Manny, who looks the worst. The lack of his medication has him nearly unconscious or maybe the medication he last had will convert him like it has converted the rest of the populous. It is impossible to tell and too risky to chance, but Max can't just shoot his best friend like a sick dog, he has to be sure; he better be sure. Salina has Manny resting on her chest and she stares at Max, terrified. She can tell just what he is thinking.

"You have to leave me behind."

Between catching their breath and keeping silent, Manny's statement echoes through the nearly empty store. Everyone winces and tries to pretend like they didn't hear that.

"You have to leave me behind." Manny repeats, drawing breath, and trying to sit up.

Salina tries to stop him, but he shakes her off.

"I'm losing myself and I know it."

"He is right." Laflamme chirps in, jumping off the counter he is perched on.

"Shut your mouth." Max growls, jumping up and gauging the shotgun.

"We will never make it to that bus if he becomes like the rest, and if he does while we're on it, can you shoot your friend?"

"Max. No. We aren't leaving Manny." Salina cries.

"We have to go; I can't stay in this gas station anymore. I want to get out." Jen cries. Tanner tries to calm her, but she pushes him off.

"I'm with Max, whatever he wants to do, I agree." Shawn in, standing up, and breaking his silent streak.

Tristan stands, checks his ammo, and looks at Brand.

Max inhales, looks around at the people he is trying to protect, and exhales. Zachary and Sarah stand still, silent, and seem to be unable to look at him. They know what is coming and so does he. Aila goes over to him and touches his chest, forcing him to look at her, trying to catch his gaze and when she does, she smiles and nods. She knows he can't shoot Manny. She knows no decision made since all this madness started has been anything less than painful, but Max has made the right ones.

Max nods and kisses Aila softly, holding the back of her head and drawing her close, he lowers his gun and pulls her in closer, living in the kiss. He separates from her, and he hands her his shotgun and walks toward Manny. He leans down and nearly whispers,

"Manny. I don't want to leave you. I thought we'd grow old and hang out on a porch and bitch about life like those two old Muppets. Man...I can't just leave you but I..." Max's whispering becomes whimpering.

"Shut up Max. I know. You don't need to say anything, but you do need to get out man. Get them out man. You need to get these people out of here and you will. You can bro, you and only you, but not if I'm slowing you down." Manny smiles as he draws Max's forehead against his.

"Take Salina." Manny whispers.

"No. I'm staying with you baby." Salina argues, trying to cut in.

"No, baby, you're not." Manny protests.

"Stop me." Salina says as she begins to weep, her arms constrictively pull him in.

"I can't let you stay Salina, Manny asked, and I can't argue." Max says, pulling at her.

"No. You don't get to decide this Max. You don't get to choose what I do. I'm going to stay. I don't want to be without him, not after all of this; not after everything I have seen." Salina says, pushing Max back, holding Manny tighter.

My poor friends.

Salina remains despite Max's pleas. No word or momentum will move her. She is as fixed as Manny's fate.

"Max. Tell Johnny that I'm sorry."

"Sorry, sorry about what?"

"About the fingernails."

The time when he cut off his fingernails and put them in my coke can without knowing that I was still drinking from it. It was horrible.

"Fingernails?"

"He will know what I'm talking about."

Oh Manny. Fight. Please fight this.

"Max. Go. Get these people out of here."

"I love you Manny."

"You too Max, you too."

Max stands up and makes motions for the group to follow him. Everyone is compliant, except Laflamme, who fiddles with something.

Max looks over at him, trying to figure out what he is doing. When Max realizes, he raises his shotgun, pointing it at Laflamme's chest.

"How the fuck are you texting?"

"What?"

"You were just texting someone. Who the fuck are you texting? I'm not going to ask a third time."

"But you haven't asked twice?"

Max runs at Laflamme, lifting him by the collar and throwing him into the glass that separates them from the cooled beverages. He shoves the barrel of the shotgun under his chin.

"Who were you texting? Our phones don't work but yours does. Start talking."

Laflamme doesn't flinch; he just grins and relaxes his body. He nuzzles his chin above the barrel and then starts to smile.

"If you're going to kill me because I was playing with my phone, shoot."

"Give me your phone."

"No."

A sound, barely a peep, but one that distracts Max begins outside the gas station. His attention is released from Laflamme, and he goes to the window.

"Fuck. We have to move. Now."

Max stares out on the once empty streets that now fill with affected, and they seem to be headed for the gas station. Max turns to Tristan,

"Keep your gun on Laflamme. Shoot if he...or she...or whatever the fuck you are..."

He points to Laflamme.

"...moves in any way before I say for her, or him, to move, fire."

Tristan without a seconds waste raises that cannon that he calls a revolver and watches Laflamme patiently, almost hungrily.

Laflamme calmly smiles. Tristan doesn't. He points his hand cannon at Laflamme and leaves it locked there. He just holds the gun so if he has to fire it'll take his head off.

Max looks back outside and watches in horror as the once vacant streets fill up.

Affected begin to gather everywhere outside, battling amongst themselves. Bodies congest side streets, main streets, and parking lots. They completely cut off any hope of crossing to the bus depot. Max sighs and realizes that he needs a distraction, and this distraction will cost him lives.

Max moves from the window and beckons everyone that can move to come close and listen; he does this without words and just body language. Everyone except Laflamme, Tristan, Manny, and Salina crowd around him and listen.

"We need to set this place on fire. We draw attention to it and go the long way around. Manny is staying behind..."

Shawn pipes up,

"You kidding me? We can't leave him here."

Max hangs his head,

"No, we can't. But he can't go on and he won't. So, let's do this for him alright?"

Zachary looks at Sarah and then at Max,

"What do we have to do?"

Max looks out at the pumps and then looks back at the group,

"We turn the pumps on and draw them in. Then we shoot. It'll light this place up and give us enough time to make it to the depot."

Tanner looks at Max, and whispers,

"What about Laflamme?"

Max looks over at Laflamme who leans on the counter, staring at Tristan,

"We'll deal with him...her...whatever the fuck it is, later. I need volunteers to start the pumps while the rest of us head out back and go around."

The group looks amongst themselves without certainty and looks back at Max, Max sighs and then speaks a sentence that collapses hope,

"We'll draw straws."

He points at a box of actual straws sitting off on the side of the counter.

All the while the group talks, Laflamme's phone vibrates in his pocket and the conversation remains one sided after Max cut him off, and Laflamme doesn't dare to check, and rightfully so, because Tristan eagerly waits for any reason to add more holes to Laflamme's body,

Silk: "How are my "friends" holding up?"

Laflamme: "Your "friends" aren't doing so well; Manny isn't going to make it."

Silk: "Keep the rest alive, those you can, and don't worry about those who won't make it. I need a way out if this all goes bad. Valentyne's friends are my friends, because as far as they know, I'm him. Where are you? I almost have the money..."

Silk: "Laflamme?"

Silk: "Laflamme?"

Silk: "Answer me."

The last several texts are more of them same, unimportant, and unanswered, and now I know why Silk looks like me. He wants out and he wants my life, but he isn't going to get it because even though he looks like me, sounds like me, they would know he isn't. They would see through him and all his lies...

Would they though Johnny? Could they actually tell the difference? You have been gone for a long time, and you didn't even come back you, you aren't the same guy who left.

I need to believe that they would know the difference...

Max, holding his head as high as he can, despite it feels as though it will fall, slumping down from the weight brought on by the shame that is his so called "solution" is the best one there is, that is, the "solution" as to how they will decide fairly who lives and who will most certainly die. He walks back to the group with the box of straws. He pops the box open and draws ten instead of twelve, writing off Manny and Salina.

He brings his pocketknife out and puts his back to the group and cuts three straws shorter than the rest. The group watches the bits of plastic straw rain down and roll away on the floor, each bit representing someone who is going to die and someone who is going to live. Max will offer these but even his fate remains up to chance, because with these bits, some long, and some short, who ever draws them while he holds them won't just decide their own fate, but his as well...

They stand around each tightly clenching their fist, unready to open it and show their straws and its length. They all know what waits for them beneath their tightly wrapped fingers, if they leave here and live longer, or die right here. They glance between each other until Max breaks and takes action. He opens his fist and has a straw that isn't short but is neither long. No one knows what it means until Tristan, who still has his gun on Laflamme, opens his hand, revealing a similar straw to Max's. This causes a chain reaction as they all slowly open their hands and show their fate for each other to see...

Three shorter straws suddenly shorten the life of three of the survivors. Jen, Brand, and Aila drew the short straws. Max goes white and goes to speak but Tanner gets his words out first.

"I'll take Aila's straw, I'm staying with Jen. If she is staying, so am I."

Max goes to protest, but he can't find the words that should go with his body language. Tanner switches places with Aila before he can say anything. Jen casts a smile at Tanner, relieved, and grateful that he doesn't want to leave her behind. Chivalry has survived when logic has died. She is comforted slightly by this and goes to Tanner's side and holds his hand.

"It's decided. Jen, you get the pumps going and Brand and Tanner will fill this lot with gasoline and when you're clear, we'll light it up. I won't shoot till you're clear but make sure you move as fast as you can. We need to make a dent and keep these fuckers occupied. Are we all on the same page?"

Tristan nods toward Laflamme.

"What about him..."

Laflamme looks at Tristan, insulted.

"Her?"

Laflamme shakes his head at Tristan, and sighs.

Tristan widens his eyes and shrugs before speaking again.

"What about Laflamme?"

"You're coming with us."

Max lifts his shotgun mid sentence and aims it at Laflamme's head.

"If I could leave you behind, I would in a heart beat, but I can't trust you'd get done what needs doing, therefore, move."

Max points at the back door as the group assembles. Manny and Salina sit up against the fridge in silence. Manny is pale and his breathing is so shallow it is almost like he isn't breathing. He is clammy and soaked in sweat. His eyelids are slits, and he looks like at any moment he'll lose consciousness, or in this case, himself. Salina is speechless at first, but forms words and stutters through them as she whispers to him. Max stops before leaving, and swallows his words instead, as he knows his goodbyes were already painful enough the first time, and that he can't bring himself to repeat them.

Shawn pulls at him while empathizing as best he can without coming off as cold; all while trying to remind Max that time isn't something they have to spare. Aila helps pull Max through the open door. Max reluctantly follows knowing for certain that this is the last time he'll ever see his best friend again, and he utilizes every increment of control he possesses to fight from breaking down. He fights the memories that try and surface, forcing them back. He frames this moment as fiction because the reality is far too painful to stomach and with that, he creates the denial that will help him keep his head where it needs to be and his thoughts on making it out. So, in turn, those thoughts will be memories, and he will one day look back and deal with the reality that is but shouldn't be.

Max, Aila, Shawn, Zachary, Sarah, Laflamme, and Tristan move behind the gas station and climb the fence to an empty walkway that waits on the other side to lead them safely to the bus depot. Jen goes into the office and looks for the key to turn the pumps on while Brand and Tanner sneak out front, prepping the pumps to fill the parking lot with gasoline.

Jen stops at the security station and watches the televisions and tries to fight the panic that overwhelms her from what she sees. Every single camera catches the countless number of affected that now fill the area. She watches them fight and struggle, but she doesn't know why. She watches them tear into each other. She watches as some of the victor's rape some of the defeated while others kill them straight out. There is no end to it. There is no logic in it. She is lost in terror as she wants to look away but can't help but watch. She doesn't even notice Brand and Tanner setting up the pumps. She suddenly snaps out of it because she hears Salina scream from the floor beneath her. She quickly smashes the buttons that turn the pumps on, and she looks back at the screen as she watches the gasoline spill into the parking lot as Brand and Tanner jam more nozzles open. She finally pulls herself together and runs downstairs.

Salina whimpers as Manny goes still. She pulls herself from under him and gets on him, shaking him.

"Manny, wake up, Manny, please...come on, don't go, Manny."

Her whimpering becomes talking and the talking quickly becomes yelling and the yelling becomes pleading.

She stops shaking him and stops crying when his eyes open and she lets out a sigh that can only express complete relief. That sigh ends abruptly when his eyes open because those eyes aren't Manny's soft brown eyes. They aren't the eyes of a loving man. Those eyes she now stares into aren't full of the life she has been a part of and loved being a part of. Those eyes that penetrate back into her eyes don't belong to him, or anyone; they are void of humanity, as though constructed from plastic, they look just like the eyes of a manikin. Her face winces painfully as her tears return rapidly, and uncontrollably so, because she knows that Manny is gone and whoever she is staring at and sitting on, isn't Manny, or anything like him. He is gone.

She screams when he moves and lunges at her, tackling her. She tries to escape his grasp, but Manny is a big guy, and his weight alone traps her. She cries out and tries to reason with him, even though she knows he is gone, and he isn't coming back. He pulls at her clothes tearing them like tissues, freeing naked flesh, and exposing her. She goes limp as he readies to dominate her.

Jen stands there frozen, watching. Salina looks up at her, defeated and still. Jen runs for the door...

Brand finishes turning on the last pump, letting the nozzle spew gasoline and snake on the ground spraying it out chaotically, soaking everything it touches. He smiles, satisfied, and moves back toward the gas station but stops as Jen breaks through the doors and sprints away. That chime goes off, the one that tells someone is entering or exiting, and in this moment, it is as loud as a church bell. Tanner drops the pump and runs after her. Brand spins in place, taking in the situation, and realizing how everything has just gone to shit and that affected now spill toward him and the gas station, and he has no way out. He draws a single smoke and taps it on his knuckles. He looks off toward the depot, and if Max didn't know any better, he was looking right down the scope that Max now watches him through.

"Fuck."

Max whispers, as he removes his eye, and looks at the big picture. He shakes off the terrible feeling of helplessness that eats at him and looks back into the scope, determined to see this through...

Salina hears the chime go, and moments later she hears it go again, and she can feel the air spill in with the affected. She can smell the gasoline. She closes her eyes, knowing the end is here, and it comes with a terrible and painful delay. She tries to stomach how unfair it is that her end comes from the hands of a former lover, her Manny. She tries to hold back the sickness, but she is losing. As she tries to accept this, fight the sickness, and pointlessly attempts to ignore the pounding penetration of each thrust from her former man turned monster, something changes. Manny stops.

Not the monster, but Manny, somehow returned, stops himself. She turns, and sees him, and his absolute sincere and apologetic expression. Signifying that he and his humanity has returned. She is at peace. He, however, is overwhelmed with terror and apology. He paints a picture of confusion and unending regret. But when he sees her smile, and what it infers, he rises to his feet, and goes to stop the affected that spill in. Manny spears the several affected that have made it in, collapsing them to the tiles below. He smashes the skull of the first one he gets his weathered hands on, and it collapses like a porcelain plate on impact. He goes after another, and hammers down on him with his fists, and his fists become just like hammers, and they do what they do best; bury nails. But in this case, the nail is a human face, and as Manny strikes down on it, he crushes and collapses orbital bones. He makes short work of the first, then the second, and after a brief struggle with the third affected, he stands victorious. He moves with a purpose that was fulfilled before he found it.

He barricades the entrance now, and he does with unbelievable speed. He uses every moveable object in reach and completes it so the affected outside, stay outside. He returns to Salina, lifts her to his chest, and cradles her as he walks from the windows, out of sight. He brings her to the office and sits with her in his arms, comforting her. She cries and tells him she loves him. He goes to apologize but she silences him with a kiss, and the kiss comforts him and doesn't end as they close their eyes...

Jen's legs push her faster and faster, like a gazelle running from a hungry lion, panicked. She doesn't have a direction or control of her emotions. She abandoned the plan. She moves with instinct and runs for survival, pure and simple. She just wants to find sanctuary somewhere far from this, as far as her legs and lungs will get her. She doesn't look back. She can't hear Tanner crying for her to wait. Jen, like her pursuers, just the embodiment of instinct, lead by adrenaline. She isn't thinking and she can't make decisions. She instead just flees, and escape is the only thing she wants or knows.

However, her pursuers are faster and hungrier. Because of this, she tastes the unpleasant pallet of asphalt as she gets caught. The impact is so hard, it nearly steals her consciousness, and in this case that wouldn't be a bad thing. Two affected tear free her pants, and when the third arrives, her shirt is gone. She tries to struggle but their strength and desire far exceed the fight she has left, and maybe even the fight she could return before expending any or all of her energy.

They prod her with flicking fingers and searching tips. One opens her mouth and drives his dirty shaft inward till it smashes into tonsils and forces a gag. Another jams his swollen appendage into her soft and clinching vagina, tearing its way in. The third forcefully invades her tiny anus, spreading the fleshy dime sized orifice into the size of dollar. If she could scream, she would, instead she sickly gags through the thrusting. Each extraction and re-entrance bring a sickness that seems completely alien and indescribably painful. She prays that through the repetitive violation, she'll get conditioned to it, and it will lessen the discomfort, but it doesn't. More affected arrive and now fight for her. One wins, and remains, and returns to ravaging her, but the others who replaced the original affected bring with them different members, with the new members, new pain. The original affected that still ravages her mouth finishes violently and abruptly, choking her airway completely as his hot and thick seminal fluid spits down into her throat. He pulls from her, spewing.

He defends himself from another who wishes to replace him, but he attempts to defend his territory. Jen gasps and quickly draws in air, trying to suck down as much as she can before further assault. She grunts as the one who invades her ass, fills her.

She looks back, disgusted, and then sees Tanner, who endures the same fate she does. He fights, but they are many, and every time he struggles, they inflict wounds that cry blood. It is submit or die. Tanner chooses death, as they collapse his skull into the cement, and he goes limp. With his passing, those who attacked him now fight to get her.

When she feels the liquid fill her last unfilled cavity, she cries. The one who terrorized her mouth is dead, and now two new affected fight for it. With a crack of a neck, she tastes the sweat of new man, as he furiously pumps in and out of her mouth. And with that terrible salty taste, she feels the fire and as it washes over her and everyone and everything around her, extinguishing her life, and all life painfully and abruptly, she gladly welcomes it...

Brand stands nearly motionless as the affected run at him from all directions. He doesn't take his eyes off the hill, not even when he lights the cigarette in his mouth. As he draws a deep breath and the smoke fills the entirety of his lungs, he moves, and salutes toward Max even though he can't know Max is there. When his hand falls, Max exhales, and squeezes the trigger. The round leaves the rifle before anyone hears the sound it makes as it does. Before the round hits, before the hungry hands of the countless affected that fall toward Brand from all directions have a chance to reach him, light gets there first; bright, blinding, and brilliantly impenetrable light fills the area. The round that hit the pump sets off a reaction that can't be explained as a chain reaction, because what follows has no pattern, no link.

Fire, explodes outward, and instantly engulfs everything, as far as the eye can see, growing, spreading as far as the gasoline has. Brand is gone. The affected are gone. Just blackened skeletal silhouettes lost somewhere in the red, removed of everything flesh and muscle. The only thing left in their place is a plume of red, orange, and yellow hues that ascend upwards and instantly fall back to where they originated.

After the fire, there is darkness, and it comes in the form of smoke. Black and grey smoke now, completely opaque and absolutely impenetrable, blanketing everything the fire did seconds ago. Finally, only ash remains; ash consisting of people and things incinerated instantly in the explosion. People and things, once solid, now flakes, and those flakes made of people now gently rain down and cover the scorched earth below.

Max vomits and sits up. While observing his friends disappear in the flame, he failed to be attentive of his immediate surroundings, and those surroundings have drastically changed. Laflamme has a gun on him, Tristan clutches his bleeding skull, Zachary and Salina hold Shawn at bay, and more importantly, Aila is in Laflamme's grasp, gasping for air, being choked violently...

COME TOGETHER, RIGHT NOW

I floor it, literally. My foot touches the floor of the car as the pedal sinks flush to it. The car jumps—no, is thrown forward—as I let my foot off the clutch, and we fly from the show room into the parking lot and the entirety of the front window follows in a hail of shards chasing us out.

I'm in the driver seat of a brand-new Camaro SS, and Janny and Becca are crammed in the back. I waste no time and feed the car the next gear as I speed down the streets toward the explosion that just lit the sky, signaling me to come. I dodge parked cars that were left to rust, and weave through them all like I'm navigating a maze. Every street I pass, affected notice me, and take after me on foot, although I am now impossible to catch, they chase.

It takes less than ten minutes to get to where the explosion originated. I see the destruction, but I bypass it, sure that nothing is left alive. However, I recognize the area, and immediately know that whoever did this, is headed for the bus depot. I don't know their plan exactly, but I have some idea. I take the highway exit that separates this former gas station and the bus depot. When I'm on the bridge above it, I slam on the breaks and stop.

I climb out ignoring the girls and with me I bring the assault rifle. I get to the wall of the overpass, and I search the area through the scope mounted on the rifle. It doesn't take long to find the only people moving, and when I see who they are and what is going on, I take aim...

"Think about what you're doing, you have nowhere to go."

Max says as he slowly rises, dropping the rifle on the ground.

Laflamme jams the end of the gun against Aila's temple and screams:

"Don't. Don't move. Just stay where you are. I am going to take her and I'm going to leave and when I know I'm safe, I'm going to let her go. If I see you follow, any of you..."

He waves the gun at the group.

"I will scatter her grey matter all over the place. Understand?"

The group nods synchronously, they all stay still, defeated, and watch as Laflamme pulls Aila away...

I inhale as he jerks her backward. He moves the gun off her for a second. When that happens, I exhale, firing.

Aila freezes as she feels liquid coat her face, speckling it. She doesn't know that Laflamme has been shot and Laflamme doesn't even know. The wounded Laflamme releases her and sprints away. Aila doesn't know that Laflamme is injured, freshly shot, and nearly incapacitated from a large caliber wound that evacuates blood rapidly, inking out and staining the ground red.

Max knows that Laflamme has been shot, and he wastes absolutely no time. As soon as he saw the wound explode and jettison blood, he is on her. He is on Aila before she even has a chance to understand the new scenario. Max doesn't know who shot Laflamme, but he doesn't care. He moves her back to the group as he watches Laflamme limp off.

Tristan doesn't just watch Laflamme leave, he chases after. He wants his gun back, but more importantly, he wants to kill Laflamme with it...

In the chaos, I rush back to the car, and leap in, greeted by two panicked women who shoot questions at me simultaneously which make answering absolutely impossible. Instead, I just hiss a "shush" sound, and gear the car, speeding toward the depot that waits just beyond the next exit.

I am like a kid on Christmas morning. Unable to wait (not even a second, though I have to) for what I know waits for me at the depot. But what waits there instead, and has waited too long, is validating and encompassing. What waits for me at that bus stop is something you can't find in a box. It isn't something that you can buy, though I would if I could. You can't put a price on it, though owning it makes you rich. It is somehow worthless and priceless at the same moment, and you could call it a paradox, but it is much easier to understand.

What waits for me there at the fucking depot, is friendship and love, it is real, and it has never changed. What waits there is everything I fought to get back and will continue to fight for, so it lives on, regardless if I do. What waits for me there are people who know me even though my face is changed and different. Who trust me, even though I'm no longer the same or could ever be again. They love me, and will always, despite everything I have done. And will forgive me, whether I requested forgiveness, deserve it, or don't. Those few who wait there, are the essence of my humanity, and my purpose for returning to it, even if only briefly. My life has meaning because of them, and because of that, I'll ensure that they don't die here.

I hit the exit, taking the corner dangerously quickly, and rejoin the empty streets of a city that is irrecoverably lost. I speed toward the depot and scan for the group I am sure heads there. As I plow through the barred chain link gates, I stop the car, cutting fresh rubber lines for twenty feet. I turn toward the girls, and smile,

"Last stop."

I open the door and get out, pointing my rifle at the threshold of the depot, and I ready myself. The depot is like a fortress, almost impenetrable from any other point other than the chain link entrance, which I now occupy and cover. It has solid concrete walls containing it on all sides, which stand at about twenty feet from ground to top and are several feet thick. Scaling them would be difficult without climbing gear because they're completely smooth. If you could climb them, you would have to bypass three feet of razor wire before climbing down to the other side. As I said, I stand between the only way in, and the only one's getting in, have to get through me.

Janny and Becca stand next to me, looking beyond the gate where I look. They remain silent for several minutes as I scan the horizon through the assault rifle, an m4 carbine with an ACOG scope.

"What're we doing? We can't stay here."

Becca breaks the silence and with it my focus through the scope.

"We're waiting for our friends."

I look back into the scope. When the landscape moves, I focus, and now I see what isn't landscape. I see a face and as it gets closer, details become visible. I recognize these details and whom they belong to. Each imperfection of skin surface tells a story. Be it a scar or even a blemish, right down to the bone structure beneath the skin, but they all do one thing; they tell a story. With this story comes an identity that I know too well, once forgotten, and now completely remembered. Through this scope I see Max's face and the emotions that his face can't help but hide. Though I should be ecstatic to see his face and find at least a moment of happiness seeing it, what his face expresses and solidifies, allows neither.

I look from his face and search for the catalyst of his urgency. When I see it, my face expresses the same emotions he does. Max, Aila, Shawn, Zachary, and Sarah run from a swarm of affected people who are so close that if any of them slowed, even for a second, they would overrun them.

I run from my spot and set up at the gate. I kneel and take aim. I don't know how many rounds I have, but I know I will make each one count, that, I'm sure. I have whatever is left of the clip that is already mounted and the two others, which hold at least thirty rounds each. That is at least sixty affected I can kill, if I don't miss, and every shot is a kill shot which I'll make sure each round is. However, that number is incremental when compared to how many affected that currently swarm toward this location. I won't even scratch the surface of their numbers, so I have to figure a way to lead the majority away, so my friends can escape, even if that means I am the bait, and the reunion has to wait indefinitely.

I fire, killing one instantly, and with one dead, more quickly follow. I go from one to another, dropping them. I pick off only the ones who pose an immediate threat to my friends who are almost at the gate. When they are close, I jump in the car, and speed off toward the affected, leaving the girls to my friends.

I pull in close to the group, blocking their pursuit, and gather their attention. They pile on my car, and I drive, slowly, herding them away from the depot. They take the bait. I find peace as they pile on and chase me, completely avoiding the depot. I leave behind my friends, the unaffected, to escape. I drive slowly at first, gathering, and killing. They beat down on my vehicle, piling on and blinding me momentarily. I shoot some off the car and allow new ones to take their place as I lead them away.

When I'm sure they all follow, I pick up speed, but I keep them following, I just don't want to be immobilized. I'm followed by a horde of affected and I lead them toward my destination, Grim Associations headquarters.

When I am close enough to the building, I pick up speed, accelerating dangerously, with only one intention, to ram this car right into the foyer of this building. I know this fight is my own but I'm bringing with me, war. I am alone in my purpose, but I come with an army of mindless drones to fight for me. I am going to remind them of what they did and in doing so, why they shouldn't have. I am revenge and all things that accompany it. I won't let them get away with what they did to me, to my friends, to the love they took from me, or the life they left for me. This ends now; it ends when I say, not when they do, and they won't escape this cemented fate. They will taste the medicine they released, however bitter or brutal, they will know it, and they will know my name. I dial Silk's phone without looking. I listen to it ring, even though it shouldn't work, but I know that mine and his will because we have the same functional frequency.

When he answers, I hang up without saying anything. I want him to know I'm coming, because I'm not just going to save Henry, I'm going to kill him, and I want him to know that death is on the way.

THE RESCUE

The engine revs when the car hits the first glass doors of the grand foyer, throwing glass and remaining frame into it. Through the foyer, the car charges, and it cuts across the polished floor, spinning in a full 360-degree circle before ramming into an empty security station and stopping. The front walkway area is completely obliterated and rearranged and now huddles together by the dying car. The engine continues to rev as if something is jammed on the accelerator.

Silk's small army comes out of the elevators in a V-formation, covering all angles of the large foyer with their large caliber assault rifles. They move in such perfect symmetry it looks like a practiced act for an international show. Rifles up and heads low. They move towards the destroyed car. Through one radio, on one soldier, a voice screams through the silence.

"It is a fucking diversion..." Silk's voice shrilly cries through the speaker of the radio and the soldier quickly muffles it,

"He is somewhere close by, find him, and fucking kill him."

I can hear the urgency smothered by fear in Silk's voice. The one covering the radio is the leader and he whispers into his mic by pressing on an apparatus attached to his throat.

"Yes, sir."

He points in one direction with two fingers. Half of the men move that way. He points another way, and the other half goes that way. He walks straight ahead, alone. The security camera follows him. Silk watches them from somewhere else in the building. What Silk and his toy soldiers don't see, is me, sitting up now, in the driver's seat, directly behind them, and the sound of the accelerator ending has them frozen as I remove my foot from the pedal. Through division, I am able to conquer.

I fire at the squad leader as I open the door. His helmet rocks off his head as his brain and skull try to leave it but are contained by its protection. He drops. I move as quickly as I can for a wall, as assault rifle fire follows me, echoing painfully as it tears up the expansive marble of Grim Associations lobby floor.

Move now or forever be in pieces, Johnny boy.

I bolt from the wall that is being collapsed by heavy counter fire, and I leap, spinning, and while sliding on my back toward the opposite wall, I empty a clip, systematically, from left to right of the team closest to me to the team farthest from me, reducing their ranks. When I hit the wall, I pull myself behind and quickly feed my cannon another loaded clip.

Well done Johnny boy, I think you may have hit someone. Aim or save the fucking ammo.

Shut the fuck up, I say aloud. I shake the voice as I get to my feet as I can hear them coming after me. I hurdle down the hallway toward the stairwell and right before I hit the door with that stupid bar across it that acts as an opening mechanism, I hear one shot, and I am propelled forward through the door with a slug imbedded in my vest.

I don't feel the pain, fuck, am I paralyzed?

I kick the door closed and through the solid kick, I have my answer. I roll away from the door as it is annihilated by gunfire. The pain in my eardrums is excruciating as they are berated unendingly because of the acoustic resonance from being in such a small space. The assault sends echoes that sound like floor drums being double kicked inside my skull.

The gunfire stops and I can hear them coming through the ringing in my ears. I roll past the shredded door and bolt up the stairs. I pull a flash bang from my belt and ready it as I climb. I hear the door come apart as someone throws themself through the dilapidated husk, sheered metal flakes that remain of its former solidity.

When I get to the next door, I kick it open, throw the flash bang behind me and roll into a wide-open office space with a dozen barren cubicles. I see all the directions through the end of my barrel before rising as I hear the flash bang explode followed instantaneously by several unharmonious screams. I see an exit on the other side of the room behind the dozen beige, grey cubicles, but I know I won't make it across in time; I have to make some sort of stand here. From behind the door, I hear gunfire, screams, and struggle, and realize that my entrance and our little battle has brought affected here.

I hope they enjoy the taste of their own medicine.

One of the toy soldiers' spills through the door, panicked and unaware of his surroundings. I am on him. I kick at his hands because they hold an MP5 navy. He drops it. I grab him by the vest and throw myself to the right of the door, chucking him. He smashes through a cubicle. I kick the door closed on another who tries to spill through and the door closes, licking his hands, removing flesh. I tumble to the side of the guy I knocked over and throw a violent hook into his chin, collapsing him close to unconsciousness. I relieve him of his MP5 and grab a fresh cartridge from his belt. Without thinking, I am already readying the gun for ammo. I press the release of the empty cartridge and feed the new one, cycling the MP5 for use. As soon as I am finished—and far too close for comfort, if comfort could exist in my life—the door swings open and I squeeze the trigger in bursts, burning two toy soldiers down before they run in. They fall, riddled with new orifices that spew hot sanguine across the floor from wounds in their legs.

I don't bother with center mass shots, and I keep firing at leg height because their legs are not protected by Kevlar like their chests, and hell, maybe I'll hit their femoral arteries in the process and completely cease future violence from them. I don't believe ceasing possibilities will have any effect; so instead, I unload the majority of the cartridge as I rise and move.

I run across the room and slide behind a cubicle as several more soldiers enter over their fallen friends, dragging them into the room so they can shut the door behind them. I can hear the thunderous swarm of affected that spill up the stairs after them, the affected that followed me here.

I can hear the soldiers desperately trying to barricade the door as a thrall of affected try to get at them. They use their downed friends to block the door, some dead and some dying. One of them breaks radio silence and screams at Silk.

"We're overrun. Valentyne is the least of our worries. We will circle around, lose the mob, and then come back..."

I stand and spray gunfire at them. The one talking on the radio drops as a stray round serrates his lower jaw and he falls gurgling. They return fire as I drop and roll toward the exit on the opposite side of the building I came from. The cubicles shred apart like paper as they fire on full automatic hoping that they hit me. I decrease my size giving them less to hit and I continue to move, tumbling closer and closer to the door. When they stop firing because they're empty, I can see them now. They have decimated the room and go to move toward me but before they can reload and resume their fire, the door behind them breaks and their human barricade fails.

I hear several grown men cry out as they're taken down. I hear the guttural struggle as they are buried by ravenous affected. I hear them scream as clothes are torn off and bones are broken. I get to the door and tear it open; I don't look back at the horror behind.

I climb the stairs, hitting every step hard, and throwing myself up to another stair and another level. I move quickly, like I know where I'm going, even when I don't. I don't know what floor Silk is keeping Alrick on. I hear the door below crash open and footsteps begin to quickly follow. I hear people fall as others climb up over them, after me. I get several more levels up this bright stairwell that is constructed from finely polished steel grate steps surrounded by deep red walls. The halogens that greet me at every level seem to get brighter and brighter. I can't climb anymore because my oxygen intake cannot compete with my staggering lungs and exhausted body. So, instead, I go through the door on this level: floor eleven.

Even though I don't have the luxury of time, I enter the hallway with the MP5 raised and vigilantly scan ahead, walking in slowly and quietly. When things appear clear, I sprint down the hallway toward an abandoned crescent desk that sits on the wall opposite of the stairwell, two big letters float above its polished surface: HR. Human resources.

Grim definitely handles its human resources.

I leap over it and spring to a stand. I turn and plant myself with perfect view of the hallway, waiting for people to come through that door. I have the barrel fixed on the door and through one eye I stare down the sights, slowing my breath to short intervals.

The door comes open and people spill out. Spilling and rushing like water, like an overflowing dam that needs draining. Each affected that squeezes through pushes over each other, fighting their way out. Some begin to congest the door as they take their own fight to the ground. Punching and clawing each other, tearing flesh and fabric, but others just push on. Those of the affected that do move on, move quickly, and they move with a purpose, that purpose, is me. I exhale as slowly as I can, fighting my lungs, that want nothing more right now than to taste air again, and again as quickly as they do, I squeeze the trigger.

The first shot punctures perfectly through the skull of the closest person who charges toward me. It ruptures cacophonously, sending off a sick popping sound that echoes loudly through the corridor. This is the only kill I consciously register because instantly after it, I don't aim; I spray left to right and unleash the entire clip, full auto. Countless fresh corpses hit the floor, sliding. Tracing with them trails of warm scarlet before settling in place. There they will remain coagulating, shot to shit, in a pool of themselves. My gun stops abruptly. No longer spraying fire and spewing fury as continuous clicking replaces it. My gun is empty and out. I'm back, seeing things in real time, one thing at a time. The chaos and timelessness of panic has subsided. I look down, greeted by the sight of a sea of empty casings that once housed bullets, which now find final residence in the bodies of my victims. I drop the empty MP5, and climb over the counter, moving into the carnage cautiously.

I draw my gun and remain ready for more. As I tip toe over all the dead, I fight the terrible truth that eats at me. Affected or not, these people were people, and I have slaughtered them. I remind myself that they are gone and despite every shred to justify my actions, these are—sorry, these were—just regular men and women. Poisoned and polluted, transformed into mindless monsters. They, like me, didn't have a choice, and they didn't deserve any of this. Whether who is to blame, I killed them and I struggle to swallow that and move on but I know I must and so I do. I swallow hard and replace guilt with purpose. I will end this, no matter what, I will. Then I hear it, a sound I have never heard before, a buzzing pulse. I turn and next to me is a large computer and on it is a device like the one Silk had, and it is attached to what appears to be a radio unit. This appears to be the HUB, the epicenter of the signal blocking all other signals. I open fire on it and the machine shorts out. I stand there smiling but I still hear that hum. The device is destroyed but the signal is still jammed. I look at my phone which is now jammed as well. Could Silk have been using this to unjam our phone signals. So, something else is jamming everyone else's, but what? How? But in my question, I have my answer that comes in the form of suspicion: it is coming from Hane.

I walk toward the stairwell, gun raised and scanning. Just before I reach the unclogged exit, I look to my right and I'm paralyzed momentarily, because through a window resting in an empty office, I see a sight that draws me in completely. I run from the corridor and stop, pressing my face to the window, and I watch in absolute fear as the streets below fill with what I can only assume are affected, and as far as I can see they herd in one direction, and that direction is…here.

A BONE LEFT TO PICK

Laflamme, weak from blood-loss and unable to continue, stops under a bike bridge. The shadow of the setting sun pulls the light from patient darkness that waits inside the passage. Laflamme doesn't notice Tristan walking rapidly up from behind and when Laflamme hears the first of his footsteps that now echo loudly inside the underpass, it is far too late.

Blood rapidly travels to Laflamme's jaw as Tristan's fist cuts across it. The hit is so solid Laflamme is instantly knocked unconscious. Before he hits the concrete below, Tristan resurrects his consciousness with another hit to the skull, just in time, as Laflamme crashes painfully to the ground. Tristan is on top of Laflamme, hammering down on his hermaphroditic face without bias. Tristan wants his gun, and he wants to kill Laflamme. Male or female, it doesn't matter; Laflamme is going to die by his hands. Tristan finds his revolver and retrieves it as Laflamme gasps for air and spits pleas for mercy through shattered teeth and drowned out gurgling.

Tristan ignores Laflamme and continues his assault, unaffected. He throws hard fists into Laflamme accurately, breaking bone and drawing blood. He withdraws briefly but returns with crushing and crippling kicks. He does this until Laflamme is tenderized and unable to move, barely hanging to consciousness and approaching breathlessness and not far from death. When he recognizes just how close Laflamme is, he stops. He takes several steps backward and draws that heavy six-shooter from his belt. He opens the chamber and checks the live rounds. He smiles uncontrollably, allowing a breathless chuckle, because he finds irony in the fact that they are called live rounds when all they are really good at is ending life.

He closes the chamber with a hard flick of his wrist, kneels down, and pulls Laflamme's face up, forcing Laflamme to eat the barrel. Tristan jams it in, past Laflamme's closed, cracked, and bloodied lips, and he doesn't stop forcing it further until Laflamme gags on it.   Laflamme coughs helplessly, gagging through saliva and blood as Tristan draws the hammer back. Tristan takes a deep breath and slowly, timelessly, exhales. Laflamme, positive that this moment, deep throating a barrel, is the end, and with that thought, closes his lashes until his lids shut out all images. Greeted by this forced darkness and the eternity of anticipation,

Laflamme cries through closed lids, and waits through warm tears.

Air, sweet and somehow frightening, suddenly fills Laflamme's gaping and freshly free mouth. Followed quickly by blood-diluted drool, spilling out over his chin, uncontrollably. He opens his lids as slowly as possible and is greeted by the absence of Tristan's immediate presence. Laflamme, confused but grateful, remains frozen in the same posture Tristan left him in and does nothing but watch as Tristan walks away, gun in hand.

Laflamme begins to laugh and cry simultaneously, completely uncontrollably, and intently watches every single step Tristan takes. When Tristan is just about out of sight, Laflamme moves, trying desperately to stand and flee in the opposite direction but as soon as Laflamme moves, something stops him. The only one that hears the shot is Tristan because the bullet fired has already exited Laflamme's skull and buried itself in the wall behind it. Laflamme lifelessly falls, returning to the place he just was, and Tristan turns again, and walks away without looking back...

FACING MY DEMONS

Silk pulls Henry down the hallway trying to juggle him and the two duffel bags he has slung over each shoulder. He has a small escort of half a dozen men. They're armed to the teeth with assault rifles, machine guns, and pistols. They're covering all directions, each pointing one of the aforementioned weapons. They're seven floors below me. What they don't know is that a large wave of affected move up the stairwell toward them. The front man of the escort stops and signals the rest to stop. Henry smashes into Silk and he catches his breath.

"Do you hear that?" One of the soldiers' whispers.

He turns his attention and that of his men toward the door they're headed for. They all raise their weapons and ready them. The door comes off as dozens spill through it. The soldiers open fire as they walk backward. Silk doesn't hesitate; instead, he pulls Henry in the opposite direction, leaving his security detail to cover their escape. Silk moves toward the elevators and slides up to the button, mashing it down. He pulls a revolver and points it over Henry, aiming it at the chaos behind him. The soldiers keep moving back.

They split into two groups to keep constant fire, mowing down everything that comes through that door. Casings sprinkle on the floor echoing discordantly in this wide birthing hallway, bouncing across the cold malachite polished floors. At every several feet, large, sanded wood doors guard uninhabited offices, and some of the affected begin to move from the firing squads' path and take shelter.

The firing squad tries to keep the group congested but they scatter, as does the gunfire, and now some of the affected move harmoniously toward the soldiers, catching them reloading.

The reloaded group retreats toward Silk and the elevators that have just opened, calling out for Silk to wait, but he ignores them as he mashes the buttons inside the metallic prison. Only one of them makes it in the elevator as the doors snap behind him, he turns and has his weapon ready. He doesn't even object to Silks decision, with remorse or any sign of it, he has no issue leaving his unit to death, or worse.

"Fucking Hane. It has to be Hane. He is here..." Silk screams, kicking the glass window of the elevator.

"Hane's out? How?" Alrick yelps, wide eyed, and his color fades completely as he accepts his situation and comprehends its reality.

"Your pet let him out."

"Valentyne did? But why?"

"Or Greyor, or whoever the fuck he thinks he is now. He killed Hanson and let Hane out. Why do you think?"

"Hane must have reached him somehow, made him do it."

"Yeah, he is good at that isn't he. I wish you would've synthesized the drug sooner, then we could've killed that guy...that thing because we wouldn't be here, in this, right now, now, would we?"

"You're blaming me? I never wanted any of this...fuck...and I told you already..." Alrick pauses, staring at himself in the large elevator mirror as it moves from level to level."...You can't synthesize what he produces...you need him to harvest the compound..."

"We have enough of the fucking drug, we don't need him." Silk screams as he throws poor Henry into the glass.

"I never wanted this...what is happening out there is wrong. What I did, wrong. Kill me Silk, but I won't do this anymore. Fuck discovery, fuck science, and fuck you. I'm done..."

"You never had or will ever have a choice, Henry; don't you get it? If you're done, here..."

Silk passes him a gun.

"Blow your fucking brains out..."

Henry takes it, considers shooting Silk, but rejects the idea as Kiryk, Silk's bodyguard, raises his assault rifle and points at his head. As if being trapped in a moving elevator wasn't bad enough, Henry quickly learns that having guns, and vastly different desires, make it worlds worse. However, all three of them are oblivious as they aren't descending, rather, they are ascending...

Henry doesn't move, he just holds the gun, Silk's gun. He lowers his head, allowing shame to jam up his brilliant mind and he listens to Silk rant like a good pet should.

Poor fucking Henry.

"We're going to use this new stuff..."

Silk shakes the bottle that freed me.

"...and you're going to synthesize the old stuff; copy it and I don't care if it kills you, you're going to do it. Because now we have the poison and the cure, and we will be fucking gods."

Ding.

Normally, the sound: "ding", used to describe the sound an elevator makes when you reach the floor you requested, is pretty anticlimactic however, in this case, my case, and unlike last time, it is like the beating of a war drum, whether or not everyone hears it that way, I fucking do.

The doors open and those inside not paying close enough attention, Silk and Kiryk, don't see me, but Henry does. When Henry smiles, a wide and natural smile, Silk knows something is very wrong. He doesn't have time to turn. I spear Kiryk from behind, forcing him into Silk, and luckily for Silk, Kiryk's trigger finger is far from itchy. He drops his rifle as he crushes Silk not only against the glass but forces Silk to break it. Henry, thankfully, avoided all of this and he is outside the elevator, Silk's gun still in hand.

Kiryk is so fast; unexpectedly and unbelievably fast, he moves between the blinks of my lids, and he kicks me, without turning, back outside the elevator and into the hall. Kiryk is bigger than me by inches and pounds and he uses that advantage like he was born to. Like everything he is and trained to be meant for this moment; the moment he beats me so quickly and so painfully, I know, and truly believe, I can't win. Luckily for me, I'm not alone.

Kiryk doesn't underestimate me, and he doesn't wait. Every move he makes, he wants to injure me as much as he can or hopefully kill me outright. Before I get back up, he kicks me in the face, which shatters teeth, and sends me backward further. Before I realize what is happening, he stomps on me. His foot stops me from getting up as I just go limp with its force. He puts his hands on my neck and tries to wrench it till it snaps but as soon as his hands start to pull, I get loose. I slide from his grasp greasily because I'm drenched from perspiration, and I get to my feet like my life depends on it and it does. I spin around him like I'm dodging a tackle and kick the back of his knee making him kneel. I clean my knuckles with the back of his skull, but he takes it and turns and dishes me several solid hits.

Kiryk and I have completely forgotten Silk and Henry, and we are lost in this fight. Fists, feet, elbows, and knees are dealt, received, or deflected so quickly it resembles flailing. It is not. We are trying to kill one another, thoughtlessly, and hastily.

I have met my match, but I'll strike it, and him.

Training is void here only because this all happens so fast, and instinct has taken over; this is kill or be killed. Training might help slightly but right now it is who makes the right sub-consciousness, instinctual, and most damaging attack, and no one normally has control of that. I don't, he doesn't, but Greyor does, and he takes over momentarily to defend and I'm helpless. Like a switch being thrown, I'm not in control, I'm a passenger in my own body but I'm awake. Greyor uses my speed and smaller size against Kiryk. Seeing everything as it comes, moving out of the way of every intended hit. He weaves, dodges, and ducks, and then with unmatched speed and power, cripples Kiryk with several haymakers and jabs. Soft, unprepared, and completely weak areas take the force of the hits. Bones crack, skin breaks, and Kiryk gets sloppy and panics. Greyor, utilizing everything I have left. Like a composer dictating his masterpiece, he doesn't miss a note. He weaves for us, and side steps every blow and when Kiryk takes a blind wild swing, Greyor moves us. Greyor moves me behind the blow, and I have Kiryk's back, I jump on him wrapping one arm around his throat from behind, and the other hand firmly holds that lock in place. Tightly my arm constricts like a snake squeezing its prey to death, crushing bone, and stealing the life from Kiryk. He begins to kneel, and

Greyor guides him, and I feel Kiryk lose consciousness and control but as he does...

You know in the movies when the hero recognizes that he had the power all along, and confidently starts kicking the bad guy's ass? This is not one of those moments. Greyor's grasp on my higher functions' fades, I'm left driving, and I crash. Greyor is once more a passenger. Kiryk sees the window, or rather, feels the change. As my footing changes and my choke relaxes, his strength returns rapidly, and he lifts me. I'm only hanging on to him.

He is like a raging bull, charging us into anything solid enough to weaken my grasp. I hit one wall; he turns us, and charges us into the opposite wall. With every impact, I lose power, and my chokehold is more like a piggyback. He charges us back into a glass pane that until just now separated this hall from what looks like a boardroom. The glass shatters instantly, exploding into sharp shards and large chunks that knick at random as they fall past us. With that last impact my hold is lost completely, and he launches me over his head and slams me down on a nearby reception desk. I'm instantly weak and winded.

He leaps up and lands on my chest with his knee, the target is my solar plexus, and he hits it dead center. My air is gone. He is straddling me, his legs tightly pin my waist down, and they lock me with his weight. He begins to pummel me, dazing me. Before I can defend myself from another hit to the face by bringing my forearms up, his hands collapse like a vice on my throat, and he begins to drain my life through cutting off my airway.

My hand searches chaotically across the surface of the desk and grabs the first thing I find, a pen. A simple ballpoint blue pen. Right now, this pen is anything but simple, it determines whether I stay conscious or not. I hold on to consciousness and hoping I don't miss, praying I hit his femoral artery. The light disappears through my blood shot eyes as I asphyxiate. This is it; I stab it into the inside of his thigh and bury it there. With the puncture and metallic smell of iron, pissing from his wound, I taste air, my vision returns just in time to see Kiryk's fist. My head smacks against the counter, and I blink from consciousness for a split second. I see darkness and in it I look for energy to bring back with me to consciousness. I look for energy I know isn't there. Like the saying: dig deep, I do. I bring back something that can't exist but now does, and it is strength.

His hands are back on my throat when I open my eyes, I can't breathe, but I'm fighting again. I try and pry his hands off, but I fail too. I try and punch at his face, but he deflects my arms with his elbows. Kiryk has me, done, and nearly out. His fingers continue to restrict and his palms force down further. He crushes down on my throat with his remaining strength intending to collapse my trachea. The strength I brought back is now gone, gone back to the depths I dug it out from. The place where I found and took it is where Greyor usually waits. His home is my mind. His rooms are my subconscious and unconscious. I look for Greyor right now because when I'm him I can access strength I can't find now, tap into chemicals for fighting and healing, and restrict pain. As I near death I understand that when I'm him, I'm unstoppable, but with access to all of those functions, I can't access emotions or memories. When I become him, I'm not me. I switch. I switch when I'm near death, preventing this situation. But now when I need him, he is gone, and I can only assume it is because our conduit has been severed by the lack of medication in my system or the introduction of the medication that could cure the affected, bring them back from the black.

Deprived of oxygen for too long and with every second that passes I feel my brain cells die, one by one. Suddenly, I see Laurie, and how she died. Silk's poison coursed through her and killed her; she died like all of his other girls. I remember Jess, sweet Jess, and I feel every last bullet puncture and pierce in and out of her, taking her from life, from me. I remember Sketch, the flames, his peeling and flaying flesh and the smell of him cooking. Then I see an image, something metal. The one thing that doesn't flash away as my life quickly vanishes, my life passing before my eyes, and that is the thought of the metal husk in my pocket. I can feel the wet mess that is his leg wound, soaking through his pants on to my side. He has already lost too much blood but not enough to get him to release me.

I go for the Zippo husk, feeling the ever so familiar touch of its shell metal on my hand, and I tear it from my pocket. In one motion, I bury it into his neck. I'm shocked, as he doesn't remove his hands, not registering the wound. Blood, thick, and spouting from a new wound, jets out and soaks my face. I remove the chunk of Zippo from his carotid artery and behind it a jet stream of blood shoots out laterally and paints the wall next to us, the wall that is several feet away. He pulls one hand off my throat and I can breathe. I thrust the bloodied shard toward his eye, and he takes his other hand off my throat to defend his right eye. The shard, which serves as a shiv now, cuts clean through his palm, and I feel a surge of energy through my coughing. I taste air again; sweet and wonderful oxygen pours into my lungs filling them wholly. With every last node of energy I possess, I strike him in the orbital bone with the chunk of Zippo husk and he topples off me. I watch him bleed out from several wounds that I've gladly left him with, defensive wounds. He stares at me from his back, blood gushing from under his hand and from his hand, and face, and leg. Even though we both know he is dying, he somehow looks at peace. Then he does something I don't understand. He nods at me, and then smiles, as though congratulating me in my victory. As though he is honored to die by my hand. I stand motionless and just watch him die, catching my breath. I inhale deeply and exhale smoothly, slowing my breathing, getting my control back. He stops breathing. His hands limply fall from the wound and from it his color bleeds out, and he is white. With his change in pigment and his complete sincere stillness, I'm sure he is dead. I turn, and absorb this, like so many others I've killed; he is a memory I choose not to forget.

Silk.

I spin around and see him come too.

Henry, that brilliant, surprisingly and suddenly courageous doctor somehow got the upper hand of our shared enemy, knocking him out. However, Henry is nowhere to be found. Silk's gun is gone, Kiryk's assault rifle is gone, and the money is gone.

Silk now fully comprehends the situation. He sees me standing over Kiryk's lifeless and very bloody corpse and walk toward him. He removes a blade and flicks it open, readying himself.

"Remember what happened the last time you tried that?" I say, wiping Kiryk's blood from my face, as I don't slow my pace toward him, which changes from walking to charging.

He lunges with the blade; I sidestep it, and bend his hand, back relieving him of it. He throws a punch across my face as the blade hits the ground, spinning out of reach. I jab him in the stomach, tearing his stitches and opening his old wound. I head-butt him, pushing him back, before leaping and punching him hard in the jaw. Before he recovers, I cut two more across his face, from left to right. Blood runs rampantly from his mouth and as he brings his head up, I kick him square in the chest, throwing him tumbling backward toward the closed elevator doors. I spear him into the closed doors, placing my shoulder into his abdomen, doing further damage to his already wounded stomach. When I step back, I realize a change in my weight, something is missing, and I instantly know what it is before I see it. I look up and see my M1911A1, staring me in the face, and in a blink I'm frozen. Behind the barrel I see the smile I have wanted nothing more than to erase from existence, his stupid smirk. He exhales as he pulls the trigger...

THE NOT SO GREAT ESCAPE

"We can't wait for him anymore." Zachary sighs.

My friends sit huddled in a city bus, inside one of the massive bus depot garage. Surrounded by dead buses on all sides, hiding them from the world outside. Zachary and Sarah sit up front talking to Max as he reads the instruction manual for the most recent bus models. Aila sits staring out the front window, silent. Shawn and Becca sit in the back of the bus, holding each other, joyously reuniting through kisses and wide teary eyes. Janny walks up and down the aisle, impatiently waiting my return. She stops, turns, and stares at Zachary.

"Can't wait for him? Of course we can."

"What about Tristan. Are we going to leave him here to?" Max says, looking up from the manual.

"You don't need to wait anymore." Aila whispers.

"Yes, yes, we do. We have to wait for Johnny, and for your friend Tristan."

"No, we don't, at least not for Tristan." Aila says a bit louder.

"We are just going to leave them here then?"

"Who are we leaving here?" Tristan says, standing next to the door.

Max, Janny, Zachary, and Sarah jump, scared. Aila doesn't move a muscle, she saw him walk into the depot. Shawn and Becca don't even recognize he has returned, and currently, probably don't care because they are just happy each other is alive.

Tristan smiles, waving his gun, and walks onto the bus, sitting down next to Zachary and Sarah.

"Thanks for waiting." He smiles, opening his gun, and throwing out the spent cartridge.

"Did you see Johnny?" Janny asks.

"No, but I killed Laflamme." Tristan says without looking at Janny, still focused on his gun.

"We have to wait...he saved me, saved me and Becca. We can't just leave him."

Max sits up, closing the manual gently, and puts his hands on his knees, looking out through the front window, searching.

"If he is out there, and alive, he will find us. We have to go, before someone else finds us. It is getting dark; we can use it for cover."

"Cover?" Janny asks through a confused shrug.

"Cover from who? Those sick people? How can we get cover from them?"

"Not them, the people keeping us locked in the city. If we can't get ahold of them, tell them we are not like the others, they'll mow us down before we get even close to them."

"What? Are you saying people are keeping us here?"

"Yeah, the rest of the world is keeping us locked up here because they don't know what is happening and they won't risk spreading it by getting close enough to know what it is. Where have you been the last three weeks?"

"Locked inside, hiding, trying to keep Becca alive."

"Understandable. Besides what is already fucked up enough about these "people", we have the rest of the world keeping us in, and in the beginning, when this first all started, there was like a militia stopping people from leaving but I think they are all gone or dead. But I want to be careful all the same. So, we have to go, we have a chance now, and we can pick up stragglers with a bus. This is our shot, and Johnny would want us to take it, trust me, I've known him my whole life and I don't want to leave him, but we have to."

Janny, reluctantly agrees, as she sits down next to Tristan and joins everyone as they watch Max go over the manual. Max looks over at Aila,

"Aila, babe, anything?"

"No babe. Nothing. We should go."

"Alright guys, lay low, I'm going to find the keys to this bad boy."

Max gets up, checks his gun, takes count of ammo, and then puts it back between his pants and belt. He steps off the bus and looks around.

Max walks between the still giants that line the depot row to row. On a normal day, this depot would be mostly empty except for the buses that no longer run or those in need of maintenance. Max laughs even though the thought isn't funny, "on a normal day". He knows that things might never return to normal. He remembers what he was doing the moment he realized everything was abnormal, or nightmarish, he was washing his car. He remembers that man, he recalls just how wrong everything was about him, and how he is different from all the rest. Max thinks, or at least believes, that man was the epicenter for this mayhem. The man that wore his friend's clothes. The man he would later know as Hane. No one told him what Hane's name was, he heard it, somehow in his thoughts like a memory reaching up to remind him. Like déjà vu, but demented, and somehow impossible, but he heard the name in his thoughts and knew that it was his.

Max had been cleaning the floor under the driver seat mat when he heard something, which later he established, was the last cry of a woman he never saw. He pulled his head out from under the steering wheel and turned down the music on his stereo. He remembers the song: *If I had a heart* by Fever Ray, that song will now haunt him, if he ever gets to hear it again, that is. Max steps out of his car, staying behind the door, using it like a shield. Suddenly, twenty feet from his car, something hits the ground hard. It must have dropped at least twenty stories. He has found the source of the scream. He walks up staring down at the fleshy and flattened mess of a woman who has fallen to her death. He hears another scream, and he turns toward it. Two men spill out of a nearby building fighting viciously. As soon as they hit the ground, one man grabs a nearby brick and crushes the others skull without hesitating.

Max was about to scream for them to stop until the brick made contact and then came the blood, so much blood. Another scream wakes him from his paralysis.

Behind him, a scream, which he turns toward, and looks for the source. A man drags a woman off the street and toward an alley, she kicks and screams but like caveman he has a firm grip of her hair, and he isn't listening. Max runs toward them, yelling.

"Hey! What the fuck do you think you're doing..."

Max gets hit from the side; he stumbles, nearly kissing the dirt but he catches himself.

"What the fuck?"

Max says trying to stand, and he gets hit again.

People are running, stampeding past him, running away from something. Not something. Everyone is running from him. Hane. People chase each other, attack each other at random, no symmetry, just chaos. Hane walks amongst them, untouched. He is a ghost. Then, something worse happens. They stop, no, not just stop, they freeze like they have been put on pause. Everyone who is attacking someone, the aggressors, stop. The victims flee. Hane stops, and a horrible and unnerving smile creeps across his achromatic, bleach white, face. The aggressors run and start to huddle around him, going to all fours like dogs. He is the epicenter, and they circle him, like the building air and debris of a tornado. Seemingly normal, complete strangers, herd to him and begin to crawl around like dogs. Hane's dogs. Enthralled by Hane, even though Hane hasn't said a word. Then it happens, Max feels sick, violated. He hears whispers and thoughts. They don't belong to him, or make sense, pressing for him to join the others, to join Hane. Max runs. He charges toward his house, kicking the door open, and screaming for Aila. She comes to him.

"Get my gun, don't ask, and get in the car."

"Babe, what's going…"

"Aila, right now."

Before she even goes to get the gun, they both cringe, hearing something that isn't noise. That sound that isn't quite sound splits into their Neocortex and resonates through every single nerve. They move, off instinct alone, knowing they have to get away from the source, they have to get as far as they can from Hane. Because this, this sound he is somehow producing, is so unsettling and surreal and it lays the way, warning of something horrible, and unstoppable coming. That he and all the horror that follows him starts here, and they know, and follow one instinct, escape. Max goes for his phone, to call for help. His phone blinks on and off, no reception. Somehow the sound is jamming cell phone signals. Max goes for the landline. Picks it up, and it is dead. Aila hands Max his shotgun, he gauges it and heads out the door with her closing closely behind.

Max and Aila jump into Max's Mazda, and they take off, leaving Hane and his massing army as far behind them as they can.

Shifting up, finding speed, Max navigates the city's congested and chaotic streets.

Downshifting to avoid pedestrians and the once human, but now changed, "affected" that pursue them. Up and down his gearshift goes, pushing his car to its absolute limit and past it. His car red lines, stabilizes, and returns to normality when he clears its core. When they finally get to the highway, pulling into the overpass, they come to a screeching stop, and the thought of escape becomes a dream. Everyone is trying to leave. Cars, row after row, as far as they can see are all going the same way, and they are all trapped. No way out. Max doesn't hesitate; he turns the car off, takes the keys and exits.

"Babe?"

Aila cries from the car.

"We gotta go on foot. Let's go, come on."

"Max, can't we just turn around?"

A loud voice booms across the horizon,

"Please stay in your vehicles, you will be evacuated accordingly, thank you for your patience."

Then a sharp screech as the voice is gone.

Then the gunshots start thunderously like horns from heaven warning rapture. Max looks down the rows of cars, and in the distance, he sees men in heavy tactical gear walk down the row, filling the cars with metal, reaping the lives of those inside. Max is frozen, watching in horror, as they grow closer and closer like rolling black clouds bringing a hurricane. They kill everything they see. Without bias and seemingly without end, they unload and then reload and then unload again. Max knows they aren't military, these are mercenaries, but for whom? Is this terrorism? Is this an invasion? Regardless, Max isn't going to wait to find out, or have his answer be bullet shaped.

"Aila, we have to go...right fucking now, leave the car."

"Why are they doing that?"

"Aila, run!"

Max grabs her, and starts to run, he runs down the skirt of the highway ramp, and leaps over the rail pulling her with him. They land hard, and bounce to their feet. They pull themselves under the overpass bridge and find a storm drain and they huddle inside.

The gunfire above is so loud, their eardrums pop, echoed painfully by the acoustics under the bridge and worsened by the tight space of the storm drain. The gunfire gets closer and closer. Max pulls Aila in tightly and cradles her as she silently weeps. The screams get louder and louder with every new pop from the barrel of an assault rifle, picking off the few that are left alive. Then, suddenly, and much worse, they stop, and silence overtakes the air. From the silence, voices spawn, and they sound proud of their slaughter,

"Point C, cleared."

Max comes back from his mind, standing in front of a wall, leaving behind the memories. His eyes bounce from each set of keys, looking for a number, and that number will match his keys to the bus they have decided to take. He is looking for a bus id number, the busses' identity, and there are so many numbers and so many keys. One set will set him free and after looking over the wall several times, he finds his set, and with it their chance of freedom.

As soon as his hand clasps the keys, Max hears something. Sound bounds quickly, snapping through the silence of the depot, startling Max aware. Max runs back toward the bus and as he gets closer, he can hear shouting, commotion, and panic.

"We have to go, now!" Zachary says, running from the other end of the bus depot.

Max runs up to the doors of the bus arriving at the same time as Zachary.

"What is it?"

"There is a group massing outside the fence, they're breaking in. If we wait any longer, we'll be stuck."

"Get in."

Max takes a head count, everyone is there, everyone but me.

"Okay, we can't wait here for him to come back, we have to go. Check your guns, save your shots, and count your stars people...we are out of here."

Max sits down, jams the key in the ignition, and turns it. The bus rumbles softly, shaking and struggling. Max looks over the dashboard, checking the gauges. Max shakes his head, exhaustively.

"We need gas."

He also sees the battery gauge but doesn't mention it and its questionable levels. Getting gas is one thing, but they don't have time to change the battery.

Tristan jumps off the bus and runs to the utility section of the depot and as he does, he shouts back,

"I saw some jerry cans over here."

"Hurry!" Max screams.

"I was planning on taking my time but if we are in a hurry, I'll be quick." Tristan yells sarcastically, sneering at Max.

Max looks back at Aila,

"Babe, can you prepare everyone."

"Yeah, okay darling."

"And babe..."

"Yeah Max?"

"I love you."

"I love you too."

Max smiles, putting his foot on the accelerator ever so slightly, gassing the bus a little; warming the engine.

Tristan returns, huffing for oxygen, nearly dragging two hazard-orange industrial size jerry cans. He drops the cans by the back of the bus, and sighs. He spins the top off the canister, pulling the funnel out, and reattaching it so it is ready to pour. He opens the buses gas cap and leaves it beside the opening. He empties the first jerry can, tosses it, watches it scatter off and then empties the second. He closes the cap to the bus, kicks the second jerry can aside, and runs up to the door, smiling.

"That'll be 120 dollars sir." He smiles, extending his hand, holding back his laughter.

"Get on the bus T."

Tristan climbs on, holds his arms up, and smiles,
"May I have your attention?"

Everyone except Max looks up at him.

"We are now departing hell, next stop: anywhere but here. Ignore the people trying to stop the bus from making its trip, they will soon be in the distance, watching as we get smaller and smaller on the horizon. Please keep your hands and feet inside the vehicle, but more importantly, enjoy your trip. Thank you."

The group stares blankly at first, but as Tristan's smile creeps over his face gently, so do their smiles slowly dawn on their faces, like the warm sun breaking the nightscape in morning.

Max throws the bus into gear and navigates the depot safely, as he comes from the hanger doors; dusk is laying the way for night. Through the twilight he can see the mass of affected at the gates, chaotically swarming each other. Max takes a deep breath, reminding himself that these aren't people anymore, they're objects in the way of freedom, and he has to just drive through them. It's "us or them", he whispers. Aila puts her hand on his shoulder with a firm yet comforting grip, he glances back at her, sorrowfully, and then turns his attention ahead.

Everyone holds on to something or someone as the bus picks up speed. The leftovers of the gate I left behind after ramming it barely hold back the affected beyond. Max pushes his foot as far as it can go downward, and then a shattering sound as they penetrate the fence, cracking the windshield, and immediately after, a sick thud, followed by countless more. Blood smears the window of the bus and the sound of crushing bone rattles Max's own, resonating deeply, and he even shuts his eyes, swallowing the sickness that tries to escape his gut. He breaks as he corners the street, avoiding two destroyed cars. He speeds up, because the several ahead can't be avoided. Thunderous is the impact as the cars spin from the buses path, taking part of the buses bumper with them. Max doesn't see the battery gauge needle decline slightly. Becca and Shawn fly from their seat. Janny tumbles out of hers, but Tristan catches her. Zachary and Sarah pin themselves into their seat and Aila holds on to Max who has the steering wheel holding him in place. The bus picks up speed as Max straightens it out. They hurdle down an empty stretch of road before hitting the highway, and suddenly, Max feels that sickness again and he sees that swarms of affected block the highway exit. Too many too count, and too many to run down, and Max needs to decide whether he chances driving through them and getting stuck or finds a new way out.

"Hold on."

Max lets go of the accelerator and readies his foot on the break, he grows closer and closer to the crowd, and right before hitting the ramp, he breaks and yanks the wheel, turning down a different road. The buses rear end collapses the front of the group, killing dozens instantly, and tossing dozens more back, toppling into each other. Blood and gore stream across the side of the bus, painting it. The needle drops more, slightly, but the battery is draining too quickly, but Max doesn't see it.

They barrel down another stretch of road, Max is trying to get back through the city core to get to the next exit, he has no idea what condition it'll be in, but it is the only option he has. That exit is right near Grim Associations' human resource building; however, the building is called the Kiron tower, and you probably won't find anything on paper that Grim Associations exists within it and operates out of it, but it does, and it is there. The dark spiraling metal and glass monstrosity is at our cities core, like a malignant tumor at the heart of a once great city, slowly killing it from inside out.

Max corners the bus, clipping several cars, and straightens out. The battery life falls ever so slightly, as though it maliciously hides the fact that it is dying. He picks up speed, heading down the last stretch before the next highway exit. He rams the remaining cars that barricade the ramp, the needle drops further, and the bus sputters for a second and he would hear it, but the impact is too loud. The bus pushes car after car out of the way, and the needle continues to fall with every moved vehicle. Sarah screams, Max looks back, and they see the still collection of thousands of affected people gathered around the tower.

"Holy fucking hell, how many people do you think that is?" Zachary gasps.

They don't move; they all just synchronously stare up at the tower.

Max looks back, and ahead he sees shapes moving toward them. He accelerates. The bus hurdles upward and then takes air, as it cleaves the remaining automobiles in the way, before crashing down on to a car graveyard that is the highway. But it is passable, and they have area to move, so Max navigates. On an open stretch Max gets speed, and he sees a group of affected running toward them from between the cars, trying to get into the way of the bus. Max floors it. He flies toward them. Then suddenly, he slams on the break, as one of the affected begins to wave their arms frantically, signaling Max to stop. They aren't affected. They are survivors. One single girl waves her arms to and fro. She seems sure that the bus will stop, that it will stop in time before running her down. Max closes his eyes because his foot is already on the floor, and the buses back end starts to slide. Smoke licks up from the rubber lines, and the bus comes to a neck jerking stop only feet from the relieved girl. Max opens his eyes, and he sees the genuine wide, white-toothed smile of a young woman, who cries in relief to see another unaffected human who isn't trying to kill her. She throws her arms down and runs around the bus toward the doors.

Right now, she is the most beautiful thing any of them have seen. She is beautiful, but she is a goddess right now because she represents hope that more got out or are still trying to. Her hair is fire red, frosted blonde at the tips, and when she smiles the world beyond her disappears behind her and she is the only thing they can see now. Her white skin is dirty but under the cake of desperation, a gorgeous milky layer awaits unblemished. They don't even hear the first thing she says, until she repeats herself,

"I'm so happy to see another face, you guys look great." She runs up the stairs of the bus and hugs Max.

"Thank you so much for stopping, oh, and not shooting me. I had a feeling that you were good people when I saw the bus. Oh, I'm rambling, I'm Sandra; it is wonderful to meet you. Do you have room for a couple more?"

Max laughs, nods, and throws his head back, welcoming her. Instead of her shaking hands, they hug her and introduce themselves. Max, wide eyed, watches people spill from hiding places and run toward the bus. About a dozen and all smiling, relieved. They have more than enough room.

"All aboard, last call for getting the fuck out of here." Tristan yells into the stillness before returning to the bus.

"Is that everyone?" Max looks back at Sandra.

She nods vigorously.

Max looks behind the people getting to know each other, and his heart drops into his guts, like he is falling to his death.

"Max, we gotta go, and I mean right now." Tristan says, pointing back beyond the bus.

Hundreds, maybe thousands of affected slowly appear in the distance, running up the streets, flooding toward the highway as the dark completely takes the day. They seem to spill out of every possible direction, all heading the same way, and Max knows it. He knows that they have been made, and if there were any better time to go, it would be right now. Max goes to accelerate and then suddenly a rumble within the bus, spouting from the exhaust, shaking to a roll, and then jerks forward and backward, and the engine suddenly just dies. Max screams "why?" at the bus, and then screams "fuck, are you kidding me?" when he sees the dashboard. The little needle dropped completely. The gauge says the battery is dead. He turns the ignition off, and then on, giving it gas. It rumbles, spits exhaust, turns over and the engine fires up. They begin to roll, and everyone goes from silent terror to tremendous relief, cheering. They get ten feet and then it stalls, and dies, and Max punches the dashboard, screaming, "Please, come on." He turns it off, and then on, it dies again. He does it again, and again, watching the remaining unbroken headlight slowly drain to dying dim. Shining the last remaining light on a very open road that is just there within reach, and then suddenly, impact...

TASTE OF HIS OWN MEDICINE

I hear an empty click, but I know my gun isn't empty, it's jammed. It has never jammed on me. I don't wait. I move the gun from my face and head-butt his. A crack, then I feel warmth run down my forehead as fresh scarlet sprays from his nose. I've broken his nose, the bridge of it to be precise. He drops my M1911A1 and clutches his face, stopping the torrent red faucet that is his nose.

I lift him by the collar, spinning us and trading spots, and then I charge toward the opposite end of the hall, lifting him from his feet. A sound punctures the air, and that sound is screaming, I'm just yelling gutturally. I have embodied rage. The world around me is gone and everything blurs, melting the scenery into liquid. We make the hallway end to end in a blink, and I ram us through the doors at its end. The dark wood of the door splinters, raining down little varnished shards.

We hit the floor below, right in the center of this grand office, him landing on his back and me landing on him. He gasps from the oxygen that is quickly evacuated by the impact. First, I think of Jess, and with that thought I lift his head, and smack it against the cold floor below. A skull fracture, concussed, his eyes spin back, and then I think of everything he has stolen from me. Everyone has hurt; I hammer him with a right fist. Everyone he has killed; I blind him with a left punch. And then I hit him so hard my knuckles split open from flesh to red and blood spills from them, the next immediate hit makes his eyes spin back. I hit him again and as my fist crumbles his orbital bone, and his flesh tears, and instantly swells, he brings his hands to defend himself from the next blow. I feel something ink down my face, drop over my lips, and then I taste blood. I spit it out quickly and I discontinue my assault, because I return to control. I know that the blood that just ran into my mouth was his. The blood carries his poison, and it courses through his veins harmless to him, deadly to everyone else. His vile ability locked inside every bodily fluid he produces, the same toxin that distorted minds and captured hearts and stopped their beats, lifeless. Then something I feared happens, I feel remorse for attacking him, and suddenly I feel bad that he is hurt. I go to console him. I try to fight it. But I can't. Every part of me yields to him. He speaks through shattered teeth, spitting out hot sanguine with a sentence.

"Get...off...me." He speaks so calmly, sure that I will.

I am about to listen to him. Jump to his command like a dog for a treat. I am at his mercy. But before I do, I feel something digging into my pocket. I instantly recognize it. It's the glass heart. I kept it to remind me that I still have one and with that memory, my heart belongs to only one other, and he killed her.

He goes to sit up and I jam my knee back onto his chest, forcing him back down effortlessly, and then I speak, and I only say one word. When I do the word seems foreign to him. A word he is not used to hearing, almost unaware that it exists. This word has as much power as the one that wields it, because some ignore this word. This word should never be ignored and because of people like him living, it will continue to be ignored. And with that word and how it sinks into him, eating its way in, fear fills him, violating and collapsing every impulse to argue. Stealing his safety and returning the terror that was just there. That word is: "No." and it hits harder than I do.

I hit him again, and he falls unconscious, but I don't stop. I just keep hitting him. I hit him so many times, my hands are numb, and occasionally I feel as though I want to stop but I ignore the feeling and continue. I lose count as his face; my face melts away. Every part that made him look like me is either broken or gone. I make damn sure that if there is any way he lives or someone finds him dead, no one will ever mistake me for him again. He doesn't get to take my life, but I get to end his and return what was stolen. He wakes up during the assault, groaning, and feebly he tries to stop me. I can't hear anything he says through the blood, broken shards, tears, and spit but even if I could, I wouldn't listen. His poison has just met the antidote. I raise my fist, intending to crush his windpipe, and before I can strike him dead, a voice cries out,

"Valentyne, stop."

I turn, startled, and hyperventilating. Henry stands there, armed, and his newfound rifle is pointed at me. He lowers it, as he knows I am not affected.

"WHY?" I scream through my erratic lungs and past the tears that well in my eyes, blinding me.

"Because this, this won't change anything, but we can. Come on."

He extends his hand. I look at it, and then down at what is left of Silk. I rise and walk toward Henry, not looking back. He removes my gun and hands it to me.

"What's wrong?"

"It jammed when he shot at me."

"Lucky you."

"Let's see."

I slide back the chamber and from it a bullet flies out. A bullet that was meant to kill me but didn't. I examine it, nothing wrong. I check the chamber, blowing into it. Nothing. There is nothing wrong with my gun. Or at least it doesn't appear to be anything wrong with it. I eject the clip. Pull back the hammer and try and dry fire it. The hammer slams down. It seems to function flawlessly. I look at the bullet, and there doesn't appear to be anything wrong with it either.

I pocket the bullet and holster my gun.

"Give me the rifle. What's in the bags?"

"Money and ammo."

"Good. We have to go; your ride is leaving."

He looks at me with raised eyebrows. I smile.

"We are getting out of here." I point toward the elevator, letting henry pass me. I stop and without turning I speak.

"Silk?" I scream at him.

I get a gurgle as a response.

I throw my combat knife near his hand, it clanks as it slides toward him, and then it spins like a bottle in place.

"Finish what I started."

I move out of the room with Henry following. I ready the AR-15, check the clip, and see that it is full and return it, and then raise it up readied.

"Come on Henry."

We run down toward the elevator.

"Any idea how we are going to get out of here?"

"Nope."

"Well, do you have a vehicle?"

"Yeah, it's waiting in the lobby, get ready to run to it when the elevator opens when we get to the ground floor, and Henry?"

"Yeah John?"

"Thank you."

We reach the elevator; I hammer the button and wait. I hear movement from floors below us, and above. Trampling toward this location. I press the button again, knowing it won't do anything and that I have been here before. I pull Henry behind me, making sure that if that elevator brings anyone down or up to us, they have to get past me and they won't, I promise as much. I am getting him out of this building and out of this city. The sound of affected coming for us seems to come from everywhere, and as they get closer and closer, they get louder and louder.

The stairwell doors on both sides of the hallway erupt open and from them, affected spill out rapidly. Before the elevator doors close, I watch as they spill into the office Silk is in. Affected men and woman are drawn to him like bees to a wanting queen.

They overwhelm him, fighting amongst each other for him, just him, nearly ignoring each other. He grabs the knife I left for him, burying it into a man's eye-socket, killing him instantly. He crawls away toward the desk as they pull at his ankles, tearing off his pants. Then his underwear is pulled like a sheet from him, exposing him. He grunts, soundlessly, as though choking, between cracked lips as one of them enters him painfully. He rams into him, freeing droplets of crimson from between his torn cheeks and widening orifice. Silks' fingernails cut into the dark wood of the desk, and he squeezes his hands till the blood is all gone and his knuckles are white, through his grip, it shakes the desk as he cries out vocally. As the affected beast of a man pumps into him, tearing him open, and pumping him with warmth, a picture falls from the desk. The picture is of Alex. He is in Alex's office. Being fucked to death, like he killed her.

He closes his eyes, defeated. And then he feels heat on his face and a sudden lock of wetness around his lips as a woman straddles herself on his mouth, grinding his face into her. She slips under him and forces him inside her.

The first penetrator pulls out and seems to defend Silk at first, but he falls through them and lands. They all attack him trying to get to Silk but stop when he stops moving. Another takes his place, pumping into Silk and pushing him into the woman. Silk fills her, without choice or the desire to do so. And as he does, he is filled. I watch through my scope, I could end this, and I'm about to until I see the glossy eyes of his first violator, and how I know them. Silk's poison, doing its work, taking another life. More and more violate and attack Silk and he disappears inside fleshy parts, bodies, and screams. Some crawl away, convulsing and die slowly, but as soon as a space or orifice is freed, it is quickly and painfully filled.

No more.

The doors close, as I remove my hand, and step back, lowering my rifle in disgust. The entire time, I wanted to open fire, but instead, I let them go and he truly got a taste of his own medicine.

But so did I...

I feel a rush of heat as my temperature rises. I'm feverish, and then my stomach gets sick as I realize, Silks poison is killing me too.

I kick the glass of the elevator mirror, shattering it with a word: "fuck." Followed by a second kick and a louder: "fuck." And then finally, I relax, staring at my shattered reflection, and whisper: "fuck."

Henry looks at me, his eyes question my actions, but he reserves his words because I think he knows whether he chooses to ignore this reality, it's there and real in all its horror.

I decline his silent question with a shake of my head and capture his attention with a lift of the gun, readying it for targets that wait for these doors to open. I watch as each floor blinks away as we descend. The churning noises from the elevator passing every floor quickly, and then the change in speed as the brakes engage. I can hear the brakes go. The sound is so loud when I know it isn't. I'm sweating and nauseous. I wipe my forehead with my arm and reposition my aim. The barrel is fixed on the closed doors. Sweat stings and blurs my vision. Questions destroy my focus, scattering my thoughts. Questions are asked. Hundreds, no, thousands of questions seem to scream at me all at once. The first being, am I going to die? The answer, I already know it, but I refrain from saying it or even thinking it. I choose how though, and it isn't going to be like this, and I'm not going anywhere until Henry escapes.

"Valentyne?"

I snap out of it.

"Yeah."

"Thanks for coming back for me."

Ding. That sound. The sound I'm coming to hate. Telling us we have landed. I take the safety off. The doors slide open; the gold of the doors disappears, exposing the lobby. My car still waits, the driver's side open. I can barely see it beyond the two dozen or so affected who now stare mindlessly at us. The second one of them moves, they're dead. I open fire without thinking. Rounds pop out, cacophonously echoing inside the small space of the elevator and the sound changes as I move forward into the lobby, growing. I bring death to everything in front of me, clearing a path from the elevator to the car. Affected explode and topple and fall away as others replace them in charging at us. I keep them back. One after the other disappears in red mist, breaking bone, and bullet cavities. Anywhere I point, death follows. Every way I go, each step I take, Henry follows, keeping his head down, and opening the duffle bag. He knows I'll need more ammo. Without asking, he extends his hand; within it a full clip awaits my reload. The first row of affected lay out on the floor without life. Their corpses are barely held together by strings of scarlet speckled flesh. A click I'm out. The affected move at me, feet from me, and I grab the clip from Henry and load it. Their hands swipe wildly, almost touching me, but before they reach me, I back step and open fire. I spray left from right, feeling hot blood paint me, as I cut them down just before they get to us.

I push forward, mowing them down. I lose count as I see nothing but red, know nothing in these moments but blood, guts, and I can't feel the glory of overcoming these insurmountable odds. There is no satisfaction here, just adrenaline and purpose. I grind my teeth, trying to keep them back, but more seem to come. They push past the dead, running and leaping without fear, just to get within reach of us. I stop moving forward, and slightly recoil, as they congest the lobby. I can't feel my arms from the constant resonating of my bones from firing this lightweight, magazine-fed, air-cooled rifle, spewing 5.56mm caliber rounds. A sound pierces the air, the sound of my gun being empty, followed by the loud and terrible sound of them getting closer and now I can hear their numbers. Their feet pound on the cold stone floor sharply, smacking over and over, like a drum roll. Then, when they are closer, they slip and tumble, and the sound of smearing liquid muffles their proximity to me.

I reach back, grab another clip that waits with Henry, and I load it as I kick one affected that has a hold of me. My hands move the speed of a lightning arc, in a flash, I'm reloaded and again pushing them back with flame and metal. Casings and bodies decorate the lobby, and I see through the chaos, with some sick focus that now there are more dead than alive. Every bullet comes with a body and with every second that passes, a step forward. I snap back, as though I'm pulled awake from some horrible nightmare, and I wish that this were just that. My body burns from the blood pumping furiously through my ventricles, systemically pulsing throughout my appendages, before returning back to my sickening heart. All fight, no flight. And then while I return to normality, slowing my pulse, and heart, I know everyone in the lobby, but Henry and I are dead. We move toward the car.

"Grab any ammo you can find." I command Henry, through short, controlled breaths, pointing at the fallen soldiers I killed earlier.

I can see outside the building, the countless affected that circle the building but stay outside it for some reason, and that reason is suddenly discovered.

I reach the driver's side door, and before I get in, I freeze.

Henry looks up at me from a crouched position as he relieves the dead of their ammo.

"Valentyne?"

I don't respond. I just stand there frozen.

"Valentyne?" He calls to me, approaching cautiously, reaching out to touch me but before his hand reaches me, I turn but not from my volition.

"Henry." A voice, my own, but carrying someone else's. My voice carries a tone, a subtle whisper that doesn't belong. I'm a puppet with its strings being pulled.

Henry knows that I am possessed; he knows I am not the one calling his name.

"Hane?"

"Hello Henry. It's been awhile. I haven't seen you since you put me in that box. That is what men do when they can't control another man, isn't it. They put him in a box and leave him there to rot. What did it feel like when you knew that they were keeping me? That you knew one day this would happen? That I was coming back. You can't kill the nature of man, especially not with drugs. These people…"

He turns my body, and points to the affected.

"They were all lost animals, we all are, just waiting to return to nature. Nature made me, and I have brought nature back to them. You can't cure nature Henry. People fight, fuck, kill, and forget. You can dress us however you please but one day, this…"

He uses me to show off the crowd like they're some prizes on a game show.

"This is what we are. Animals. Civilization was an invention to quell the chaos that waits to breed in us all. It was my company. You all took it from me. You wanted to give it a purpose. I just wanted my children back."

My mind returns, and with-it questions, questions I haven't asked because the answer is too dark to shed light on. Where are all the children? Was Hanson being literal when he said Hane was the Pied Piper? I feel a tingle in my body, a shred of discontent that turns into resistance. I'm fighting for control.

"Henry, I can see you're disgusted by me, and all of this. You believe that I am evil, that this, all of this is wrong, but you are what is wrong...you and this society and your false sense of superiority. Trying to cure what nature intended for us, like we are sick. Men like you have tried to change the world and failed. Men like me have gotten close but failed. Men you call horrible. Men you call monsters. But what our race fails to see is we are the monsters, and we are the worst kinds because we choose to kill or cure. Nature doesn't choose, it just is the way it is, and it created me to return us to our former greatness. I am our cure. Not your drugs or your technology. Just me."

"You're truly insane Hane."

"I knew you'd say that, I didn't have to read your mind...Henry. Come here."

Henry can feel Hane try to overtake him, attempting to control him. His words, whispers that crawl like a thousand spiders across his gray matter. Probing and digging in, waiting to breed. Henry knows this feeling; Hane has done this to him before, made him do horrible things. However, this time it is different, and Henry knows it, and at the same moment, so does Hane.

Maybe the medication Henry took prevents Hane's abilities...

"What's this? Protest? A spine? Where did you get this? How did you get this? Valentyne, bring him to me."

I don't move, and I can feel Hane, pushing me to get Henry, but I fight it. I shake it off, like a vicious craving that has had me for years, dictating my every action. I shake him off. But I don't move, I just fight him from moving me.

In my head, a voice cuts in, Hane's voice is all I can hear.

"Kill him, kill him like all the other unaffected you have killed..."

I fight him, his control, and his words.

"That's right, who do you think you have been killing? Those weren't policies; they were immune to what the company was pushing. They didn't fit into the plan, so they were taken care of, by you. You had a hand in all this. Controlled by him..."

I raise the AR-15 at Henry, shaking; compelled to shoot but do everything I can to stop myself from doing just that. The sick sweat pours down my cheeks. My lids are heavy, but I can't blink. My stomach churns sick but I can't settle it. All I can hear is Hane.

"Remember your roll reaper. You're told to do something, and it is done. All those years ago, you tried to kill me, but they stopped you. He stopped you. And because of him, you lost everything. End him."

I can feel him deep in my mind, he's been here before, and it is like he belongs here; like he owns it. He shows me things. Memories. Memories that are not mine. Wait, no, he isn't in my mind. I'm in his. I see things that can't be.

First, I see him in a town, not a city, and I see people, hundreds of miserable people, and the misery stems from Hane. I see him take their children far away, and no one ever sees them again. He has done this before, so many times before.

Jump forward. I see him in the middle of wars that were over 40 years before I was born. I see Hane there. He wears a grey uniform with an armband. He is of important military rank for a foreign country. He has done horrible things, made people do horrible things. He is close to the man who started this war, so close he could've started it himself. Whispering into his leader's ear, controlling him completely. Then, the bombs drop. He is on the run. He doesn't get far. He meets my gun, wielded by a soldier. The soldier is armed. I see my gun, but not my gun. My gun before it was scrapped into parts, parts I used to rebuild what is my gun today. I see it fire and watch a bullet leave it. I feel the bullet hit Hane. Deflagrating inside his body, pushing his organs apart, and moving them away from where they should be. The one, who shot him, is a faceless man, but I know that is what will be my gun. In this memory, Hane is dying, and being captured.

I'm pulled from this, transported to the moment I laid my own eyes on him. I hear his words.

"I know that gun, it's tried to kill me before."

I wanted so badly to shoot him, but I wasn't myself. I wasn't in control, just like now.

My finger starts to squeeze the trigger. Henry walks toward me. Somehow sure I won't shoot. Henry can't see Hane. Only hear him speak. Speak through the army he has outside. Henry looks at me, past the barrel and speaks, and his words cut through the cloud of my mind, like a freshly sharpened blade through fat.

"Fight him. Fight him like you have fought everyone and everything else."

I blink, as my finger moves off the trigger.

Henry moves forward past the gun, grabbing something from my vest. He lobs it into the crowd.

He extends his palm, in it a pin, and he speaks.

"It is time to leave."

We are in the car, I'm starting it, and he ducks into the passenger seat. Behind us, the affected are thrown from the entrance of the lobby. Cut apart in a concussive blast from a freshly detonated grenade. A brand-new paved path of broken and bloodied affected carve our escape. From the rear-view mirror, I see them scatter and attempt to reform the sea that blocked all exits. And I see Hane, on the ground, on all fours, regaining consciousness.

I put the car in reverse and topple everyone in the way, guiding us out backwards. We hit the street, and I put it in first gear, spinning the wheel so the car points in the right direction: the highway. I pound the gas, accelerating quickly. The RPM climbs licking at the red, and I shift, as the torque throws us forward. We run down countless affected that try and block us. Toppling them dead.

I clear the crowd, shifting quickly, and we fly toward the highway, dodging dead cars, swerving around them. On the ramp, I redline again, flying upward. I hit the top of the ramp, momentarily separating from the ground. The car smashes down, sparks fly from under the car as it fish tails and then straightens out just as we are greeted by more affected running toward a bus full of people, a stalled bus a driver furiously tries to start. I gun it toward the bus, cutting down the affected in my way, aiming for its back end, and I pray the bus is in neutral. Max dammit; please say you have that beast in neutral.

Impact...

THE LONG GOODBYE

On impact, I'm thrown forward into the steering wheel and Henry ricochets of the dash. The people on the bus are tossed forward, and the bus rolls. Shards of the Camaro's grill, headlamps, and frame explode. The bus's rear, billboard, and brake lights are obliterated. The bus rolls forward, and when the Camaro finds the ground again, I give the accelerator everything. The Camaro slides from left to right as I begin to push the bus forward, faster and farther. I run over the prismatic debris of both vehicles and stare forward, looking for Max. I need him to recognize me and know what I am doing. I can't see him, not past the crowd that congests the bus.

I bear down hard on the gas pedal and the bus moves forward, faster and faster. I know the bus is dead because it is the only reason it is sitting here. Max and I have kick started countless vehicles together, all we have to do is get this one to about 30/km an hour and he just needs to throw it into gear, that should start the engine, and he could drive on his own. I look at the speedometer; it reads 10/km an hour, even though my rpm is redlining. I hear a large horn blaring,

Max is trying to signal me, and that is when my driver's side window bursts just as Henry yells for me to watch out.

An arm grabs at me, ripping at my larynx. I un-holster my USP tactical and unload it into the body belonging to the arm that tries to choke me. A clip is gone in seconds, as is the arm, but I lose control of the Camaro. I watch the speedometer drop as I straighten out, reconnecting with the bus, and accelerating. I look at the rearview, and it is blanked out by affected that are catching up to us.

"Henry! The wheel! Just keep us straight..."

I reach back and rescue the AR-15 from the backseat, with it firmly in my hands; I turn my upper body against the seat and point the rifle at the rear window, all while never letting up on the gas pedal. The speedometer reaches 15/km an hour. I fire in bursts. The back window comes off in the first second, shards of glass paint the streets, and I cut down the closest affected to the car and bus. I can't count the number of affected that are there because there are too many to count with so little concentration, let alone differentiate between the ones who have caught up to us and the ones who are climbing on the bus or on the Camaro. I just point and fire. When one falls, I look for another, and I repeat this mindless repetition until my rifle runs out.

Speak of the devil, click, I'm out. I toss the rifle to Henry and turn to retake the wheel. I glance at the speedometer: 18/km an hour, still pushing the bus forward, and I postulate that if I am moving 18/km an hour while pushing the bus, then the bus may be moving slower or faster, and I realize I'm terrible with math.

Max looks down at the speedometer, swears, and looks up at the road ahead that taunts him with freedom. He looks back through the rearview mirror, grasping for a glimpse of me, and swears again when he doesn't get it.

"Fuck! Keep them off the bus! Use whatever you can, but get them off, we can't slow down."

He screams back at the passengers who are already panicked, moving from their seats to either stare out or remove the hands that hang from the windows. His cries are unheard as everyone on the bus does their own thing to deal with the situation. Aila, however, stays at his side, speechless and calm. She believes in Max, believes that everything is going to be okay, and that being by his side is the only place she needs to be.

Max, without showing it, fights the panic that eats at his very core and pushes for him to grab gear shaft and shift from neutral to first gear, knowing full well that if there isn't enough speed that the bus will come to a dead stop, and all life trying to move it will also come to a dead stop because there isn't going to be a second try. Then it dawns on him that even at the right speed there is no guarantee that the kick-start will work and start the engine. He and I have done this enough times to know, even with the right conditions, engine life isn't guaranteed. He salivates and sweats and nearly screams knowing that there is only one chance to get this bus going, if that, and worse, that nothing he can do will speed up the process. He just has to be patient, which for the moment, is a concept so foreign it may as well be something torn from the pages of a fantasy story.

He suddenly finds a strange peace in this dark and seemingly doomed moment; somehow, he finds hope in memories of his life, and ours together. He realizes in this terrible moment, unfair as it is, it is only a mirror of every other moment of maybes and certainties in life. Because nothing, absolutely nothing, no matter how small or big, or repeated time and time again, is ever, despite previous outcomes, is ever guaranteed.

Max waits, in a state of calm that has no word, and happily revisits memories of kick-starting engines we have had. Max taught me how to ride a bike, rollerblade, start and drive a car, and hell, he even taught me how to hot-wire his truck with nothing but a Philips head screwdriver. Max and I have been best friends for as long as we have had memories. He was the first person I met in this city, but more importantly, I have known him as long as I could form memories. We may not share the same blood, but we are family. We have been through thick and thin, heaven and hell, and any situation you could possibly imagine and somehow came out mostly unscathed on the other side together. We survived distance, age, employment, significant others, hell, even death, but here we are, braving yet another trial together. With this thought, Max is unwavering and completely focused. He is untouched, uninhibited, and indomitable as his hand rests and waits for the speedometer to get where it needs to be.

I, however, unfortunate as always, do not share Max's Zen-like state. I fight, using every last iota of energy I possess just to keep the motion of the Camaro and bus forward and accelerating, ever climbing toward the goal of transportation independency.

I am sweating through every pore as I battle a sickness that will inevitably kill me, and I know with certainty that no cure exists for it. I wage war against time because I know mine is up, even though I don't know when or how soon, but I appreciate every second I get as a win. I disregard and challenge the very laws of physics as I push this bus with an object half its size. I do all of this without considering what follows. I don't waste thought on the: "what if this doesn't work". I just bask in the disputable chance of success, ignoring the odds completely. To me, this will work, without fail. I know. Some would refer to this sensation as blind faith. I am not blind or religious. I know faith as a concept, and I know the concept as empowering positive outcome. I can't rely on an icon or deity that may or may not exist. Therefore, I rely on myself and empower the idea that I will prevail. I am my own god, and I control my own future.

20/km an hour is what the Camaro reads. The affected that aren't attached to the bus or the Camaro begin to slow and stop, but they don't battle amongst themselves like they should in the affected state. No, they are attachments of Hane and wait as he does.

"Henry, take the ammo out of the bag, and strap the bag to yourself."

I say, nearly screaming as I shoot the clinging affected who attached themselves to the Camaro. I do this sloppily, spraying through the rifle, using anything in the car to compensate for the recoil. I do this because I don't let go of the wheel. Henry complies without argument, dumping the ammo out and zipping closed the duffle bag that overflows with bills.

22/km an hour...

I gear to second, the Camaro shakes, and with the change the front-end digs under the rear of the bus. The bus picks up speed without the constant back and forth that belongs to inertia, this bus has momentum.

27/km an hour...

I realize this isn't that fast and that in short distances an average person could run this speed, however, this speed is more than adequate because the people chasing, despite the aberrations they have become, can't maintain a speed close enough to catch up. Also, this speed, however slow, is almost fast enough to try a kick-start.

I gun it, driving the engine red and stay in this gear, up until the little gauge arrow spasms. As it rocks up and down, screaming for me to change gears, I just stare at it. In a moment I can only describe as eternity, I shift into a higher gear and suddenly the torque compensates, and the Camaro spears forward and with it, the bus separates, escaping the Camaro.

30/km an hour...

I red line again, and ram into the bus, throwing it into the next gear. The bus flies forward, rolling steadily, and begins to pick up speed on its own from a slight decline in the highway. I rev again, but my car sputters, and I compensate by downshifting. My bumper is still trapped under the rear end of the bus.

36/km an hour...

Max exhales, pressing the clutch, and he closes his eyes and everything disappears around him. Within that, he forces his right hand forward and to the right from the middle of the gear box, guided only by hope, and he shifts the bus from neutral to first. He does it so flawlessly, notching from no gear to a gear without any natural resistance from the transmission, as though he has driven this bus and understands every segment of it.

Max shifts it into first and without impediment or stutter that belongs to the kick-start, the engine starts, and Max screams as he accelerates. He opens his eyes, and with his newfound sight, hope. He watches the gauges on the dash and how the alternator feeds the battery and in turn the battery finds life and lights the dashboard.

The bus speeds up, disconnecting powerfully from me, severing our symbiotic relationship completely, and leaves me in its dust, triumphantly. Victoriously I scream, Max screams, and the people in the bus scream, joyfully and harmoniously, celebrating the same thing, freedom. I watch and appreciate, frozen in time, just watching as the bus speeds away. I let go of the gas, falling back, reading myself to watch it leave, and I am relieved to know that in all of this horror, and loss, I personally saved the people I love.

However, like all things me, the victory is snatched away almost instantly with the realization that the bus is one passenger short which leaves a new problem. I need Henry on that bus. If Henry isn't on that bus, then the cure isn't on that bus, and without the cure, this may never end. I need that, I need to get Henry on that bus, and I will. I cram my foot down and hear the roar of the engine, it responds without a sign that it has been through the hell I have already forced it to travel. It responds like it hasn't seen the road but knows it is about to. It embraces the challenge and overcomes it, because this car does exactly what cars were created to do, it drives.

"Valentyne, you don't look good."

"I know Henry."

"You're dying, aren't you?"

"That's right Henry. You aren't though, not here, not for a while."

"There has to be a cure. I can make one...all I need is..."

"Henry, there isn't time. You know that. You don't have any equipment. Henry don't be stupid. Listen, you're getting on that bus, but it won't be easy, you need to do everything I say, alright?"

"Yes, of course, but you're coming, right?"

"No, Henry, I'm not and you know that."

"Valentyne, you don't have to die here, alone."

"Yes, I do Henry."

"How am I getting on that bus while it's moving?"

I drive up next to the bus, getting as close to the front door as I can, and I look up at Max. He opens the doors and screams at me,

"God you're ugly, what's up?" He says, smiling, glancing from me to the road ahead.

"Keep her straight, I want to try something."

He nods, trusting me. I'm going to attempt something I have only seen in movies but have always wanted to try. I speed up, passing the bus, and I open my door, holding it ajar with my foot. I glance back and make sure that I am still beside the bus and not directly in front of it. I jam on the breaks, the car tires lock, and the car screeches to a rolling stop. Just before the front end of the bus makes contact with the open door, I pull away my foot. The driver side door of my car is savagely pulled from its hinges, tossed away effortlessly just like it happens in the movies, but what follows hasn't been depicted in the movies. The car is thrown violently away, to the right side of the road, and starts to spin uncontrollably even as

I try to even out. When I finally do, straightening out and accelerating after the bus, I shake my head, trying to throw away the resonation that ripples inside my bones from the inertia caused by the collision that I didn't anticipate. The world outside the Camaro nips at my skin as I pick up speed and retake my position to the bus. Max greets me shaking his head and rolling his eyes, solidifying the stupidity of my actions with disapproval. He smiles, and nods, commending me. He even laughs, although I can't hear him, I can see he is. He screams down at me,

"What now smart guy?"

"Get people to help pull this guy on the bus."

"What?" He screams, barely able to hear his own voice. So, I repeat myself, using body language and yell louder.

"Get people to help pull this guy on the bus."

He shouts back and several familiar faces appear and walk down the stairs, cautiously awaiting the new passenger.

"Henry, climb across me and reach for their hands."

"What?" He screams at me because the inside of the Camaro is as deafening as the outside world that flicks by.

"You need to reach out and let them pull you on the bus. Climb over me and reach for them."

I nod towards the open mouth that was once my door. He tightens the bag around him and awkwardly climbs across me. Tristan, Shawn, and Zachary reach out and greet his arms with theirs while I keep the car straight despite with his body in front of me, I am blind, and barely able to hold the wheel. They tug and Henry is torn from the Camaro, and as he is, I let go of the wheel momentarily to help him. The Camaro smashes into the bus and then bounces away, I grab the wheel, and I regain control, as I straighten it out, and accelerate to rejoin the bus.

"Just like the movies eh Johnny?"

"Hell, yeah bro!"

"Your turn, keep her straight, we will get you." Max yells. Smiling brightly. Henry stands and tries to say something, screaming at me.

"Johnny, you're the...the new medication its part...you...it is the reason Hane couldn't control me...You are the cu..."

I get bits but I dismiss him and scream for Max and Tristan pulls Henry into the aisle of the bus so I can talk to him.

"No Max, I'm not coming with you."

"What?" He says, shocked, and nearly disregards my words as a joke.

"I'm not coming. You have to keep going...it is already too late for me Max; it always has been. Do not stop this bus, no matter what, you have to keep going and get as far away from here as you can. Just get out. I love you Max."

"John. Fuck off. You're coming. Don't be stupid. If I have to drag your ass out of that car and pull you on here myself, I will."

"Max! I can't. You need to go. Let me go bro. I am sorry. But you need to let me go."

"Johnny, no, I don't. Just take their hands..."

The guys grab at me, but I pull away.

"You don't need to stay here. You can live. With us, and you can tell your story, the truth. You aren't dead, you never were. Come on man. Please…"

"Max, you buried me already. Let me go bro and live your life, for me, for her, and more importantly, for you. I love you bro but this ride isn't for me. Goodbye Max."

Max unbuckles himself and pushes past them, the bus swerves without a driver, and Tristan grabs the wheel and steadies it. Max stretches across the gap and grabs me, almost pulling me from my seat and if I weren't attached to it, it would've worked. Shawn and Zachary grab at him, holding on, trying to pull him back but they can't, so they just hold on.

"Johnny! No…"

I whisper in his face, the cold sick sweat stings my watering eyes, and I speak slowly. The world around us quiets and he can hear each word perfectly and each one hurts more than the next.

"Let me go bro…you just need to let me go. I have to finish this, and you have to get these people out of here. It is already too late for me; I have something that I won't come back from. I don't want to die on a bus leaving, I want to die killing the people who did this to me, to us, to her; I want to go down swinging. Max, I love you, it is time to let me go…"

With that he stares at me, which only takes seconds, but I feel like this look lasts minutes and with that look he lets me go.

I slam on the breaks and disappear from his grasp and view. The bus hurdles away. I see Max move, trying to stop the bus but everyone grabs him to restrain him. I watch as the bus goes on, growing smaller and smaller in the distance. The remaining taillight glow, like a ruby eye, gets weaker and weaker as the bus gets farther and farther until it is stolen by the night. I put the car in park and unbuckle myself. I reload the rifle and load my vest. I turn the car around, speed back toward the city, toward Hane. Toward the end.

MY OWN WAR

I see the horde in the distance ahead, I make a mental note of my ammo, and it is as follows: one full cartridge in the AR-15, one grenade for the launcher attached to the rifle, one grenade in my vest, two clips of .45 ammo for each handgun and that includes the clip I need to load to replace my empty USP tactical side arm, and one folding baton. Regardless of this being enough, I will reach Hane, and somehow, I will kill him.

I gain speed as I shift to the sixth and final gear, hurtling toward the barricade of abandoned and destroyed cars that congest the mouth of the highway exit. I take my foot from the gas pedal and glide toward it. I ready myself as the car rapidly loses speed. When I am within fifty feet of the barrier, I drop from the car, and roll. I painfully hit the road and tumble, spinning uncontrollably, end over end. I don't have the ability or focus to see the Camaro collide with another car because I have yet to stop. As I slow, I try and stand and compose myself. I pop up, dizzily, and direct the rifle, awaiting targets. The Camaro melds into the barrier, loudly, and explosively. It joins the rest of the abandoned and broken cars, but it does so brightly, as it ignites in flames upon impact, illuminating the darkness of the dead city in a fireball of shards and heat.

I move forward, strafing and searching for movement. I lower my rifle as I find none and sprint forward. This becomes my second mistake in a series of mistakes, because my first mistake is coming back. I'm thrown backward by force. The force belongs to a round, fired from a gun that is held, but not aimed, by the person who pulled the trigger. The physical shooter is a random affected man, chosen by Hane to carry out the shooting but irresponsible and incapable of it on his own because he is nothing but instinct and desire. Regardless, when that shot is fired and the bullet hits my vest, I turn and return fire. The shooter drops the rifle because I retaliated with a kill shot, thoughtlessly, however precise. His head comes off and he drops. Two more affected pop out, armed, and begin to fire. I drop down and unleash the fully automatic capabilities of the AR-15 severing them at the knees. They drop and I quickly aim and fire two shots. One hits the man on the left in the cheekbone, splintering his skull in a bloody pop. The other hits the woman on the right, just above her collarbone, and her head sickly hangs onto her torso from sinew like strands.

Immediately after that, affected seem to pour from the nothingness toward me, from every direction and every crevasse they appear. I respond, halting every one that gets to close, controlling my fire and ending each life. I know that deep down, they are sick, and unaware of their actions but their actions, unrealized by them or not, will halt or hurt me and because of that, I end them. I don't excuse my actions or even try. I continue, thoughtlessly, better yet robotically, because I am cool and without remorse or the intention of slowing down. Rehearsing motions and actions that I know, with one hundred percent certainty through killing each target that it will forward me toward my destination. I end the journey of every life that moves toward me in a thoughtless blink, regardless of their individuality. Age, sex, or the possibility that they could be cured and return to normality doesn't slow me, I kill them. I know, without doubt, I will reach my destination because I kill them so quickly, without question or challenge or concern for what could be. I don't hesitate and because I don't, I will reach Hane.

I will eventually make it to Hane because opinions and morality are irrelevant here and more so, they would get me killed or worse. That is the sad but undeniable truth. Second-guessing gets you dead, or worse. If you don't follow your instinct immediately— no, not immediately, but more precisely— instantaneously, you die. When logic has collapsed and chaos replaces it, if you pause, even for a second, you are dead, or worse.

I hear that click, that horribly loud and sobering click. I grab the launcher trigger; turn my rifle at the barrier, and fire. An object, larger than a bullet, but no bigger than your fist, tears from the second barrel and hits the barrier carrying a small thumping noise upon impact. I drop the rifle and charge toward cover as that small thumping noise becomes a deafening explosion that tears the barrier apart and sends fire and metal outward concussively. It tears everything in a twenty-foot radius to shreds, incinerating metal and flesh alike, in a bright and powerful flash.

When my hearing returns, I pull out my pistols, checking to see if they're loaded, and when I am certain they are, I rise. I stand and aim, searching for a target, and find it. Through the fire, six affected charge toward me, forced forward by Hane because the affected are only instinct, they wouldn't do this, because this goes against self-preservation. I aim from one barrel to the next, popping rounds off, and back stepping as my ignited enemies get closer and closer. I kill each of them, carefully aiming. Shooting round for round between the M1911A1 and the USP tactical. I do my best not to waste bullets, but they don't just charge at me like the mindless drones they should be, they scatter, using logical tactics. Because of this, I run out of both clips after killing all six. I drop my USP because I know I have only one clip of .45 caliber ammo, and I would take my gun over the USP any day. I empty the M1911A1 and reload it within the same motion just as more affected swarm toward me. I kill one but as I realize that there are more affected than I have bullets, I pull the grenade from my vest, pull the pin and toss it into the core of the swarm. I holster my gun and run the opposite direction, diving behind a nearby car, and when I hit the ground behind it, I feel blood run down my chest from under my vest from the gunshot. I hear the cacophonous explosion as the grenade detonates and I feel the gore of countless affected coat me. Once solid and now mostly liquid paints me.

I rise aiming my gun; greeted by the light given off by the destruction from the grenade, illuminating everything that once belonged to the night. I now see Hane, off in the distance, reveling in the carnage. He sends the last of the affected after me. I greet them each with a bullet and with every bullet I fire, I drop one after the other, and after my clip is out, more still come. I grasp for my asp, take it out and unfold it. I hit one who leaps at me with a knife, I sidestep him, collapse his face and retrieve his knife, holding it so the hilt is in my hand and the blade is under my fist. I swing at the next affected in proximity to me crossing the shaft across the affected's jaw, shattering it. I swipe up and cut open the throat of another affected. Blood spews from the wound as I crush my asp down on the top of his skull, crumbling it. An affected woman jams her fingers at me, catching my eye. I back step, knocking her from me. I blink through the blood that blinds me. I swipe and slash as two others jump at me, wounding them so they withdraw momentarily. I throw my knife through the two I just wounded that now flee; it cuts through the air sharply before impaling the chest plate of the woman who damaged my eye. She drops, dead. And with her, no more come.

I shake my head, clearing the blood from my vision, and I walk on.

I walk toward Hane, empty of ammo, absent from all my weapons except my gun. The same gun, or at least parts of it, that at some point, at some time, nearly killed him. But my gun, rebuilt, unloaded, and different, now prepares to face him once more. I have one bullet to load into it. That is all I need. One round for one man. I draw forth the round from my pocket, the same round that failed to fire and kill me, and I chamber it, ready for fire. I get within arm's reach of him before he speaks and stops me.

"Stop."

And I do, whether I want to or not. I do as I am told. All while a part of me screams for me to disobey…

Elsewhere the bus full of my friends hurtles toward a barrier and that barrier is guarded by heavily armed forces who will not let them pass because of their supposed affliction that they can't allow to spread. The bus continues unaware. The posted soldiers see them before anyone on the bus sees them. They request orders. They ask what they should do and how they should handle things. They wait patiently for the radio silence to break while the bus gets closer and closer. They have orders that they came with, and those orders told them to eradicate anything trying to leave the barrier. Those orders were given before they arrived here at the barrier and they haven't heard anything else, of any kind, since. They raise their weapons preparing to fire. One of them gets on the radio, turning it into a megaphone, and orders them to stop but nothing but static comes through the speaker. The bus continues and doesn't hear it...

Hane walks toward me, raising his hands. I raise my gun but am again paralyzed by his voice.

"Here we are again...someone else, with the same gun, trying to kill me. Did you know that doing the same thing again and again and expecting a different result is the definition of insanity? Therefore, you are insane. I, however, am not. I expect the same result. I have done the same thing again and again, before you, before everything you know, and what I desired was rewarded the same result. I always get the same result and want nothing more. Regardless of my ability to succeed, everyone that opposed me always formulated the same conclusion: that I am insane, but I still, despite all of them and their shared indifference, continue to live while they always die."

I stand there, motionless, gun raised, frozen and helpless.

He examines me, his hairless brow line jumps and he begins to smile.

"You're dying Johnny. Silk's talent, his poison. It is killing you. Join me and I can heal you."

I can feel him creeping around my mind. He begins to change things, like my mind is a circuit board; he begins to reconnect severed lines. With each line he repairs, I remember something I had forgotten, whether I want to or not. As he bonds back broken pieces of my mind, I feel strength, and health. He stops suddenly. As though he has discovered something, a black and secret recess in my mind, and he withdraws.

"So why resist me? Why not help me stop your pain? Why do you keep fighting when you have nothing left? You're a soldier without a war. A lover without love. You have lost everything you have ever wanted. So why not join me? You resist because of that place you won't let me in, what is there Johnny? Show me what is in that blackness you keep up there… Your mind is a prison, worse than any imaginable place or factual residence, and I can't begin to comprehend why you fight me or why you fight to stay alive. Your existence is misery John. Beyond that. You have so many questions rattling around up there and you know they won't be answered but you ask them again and again regardless. To what end? What is the point, Johnny? My god, Johnny, so many hopes and dreams in here that will never be, gone long ago, lost or stolen, and no hope of ever coming true. You're in hell..."

The bus still rolls forward, the occupants see the barrier and the guns that point at them. Max gets on the PA and screams through it, trying to show the soldiers that they are not affected. Trying to stop their fire. Nothing but static and silence comes through. The same comes from the barrier, through the speaker, voiceless commands to desist their journey. A soldier screams for the bus to go back, but the air is dead quiet.

He walks around in the sickness that is my psyche, and I can do nothing to stop him. He sees and knows everything. This is the terrible reality, that what he can do isn't as unbelievable as it sounds. Every one of us has had a person in our life that could pull our strings or has been able to burrow so far that no matter what we did, we couldn't rid ourselves of them. So, now, imagine if someone could do that to anyone, and if you can imagine that person, imagine them as the person that hurt you the most and then make them worse. That is Hane. He is everything that he shouldn't be. He is the evil that every story depicts. He is every hate that exists. He is everything wrong with the world, even though everyone shares the same opinion that what he is needs to end and go, and despite how powerful that desire to rid the world of him is, he is there, manifesting it and going absolutely nowhere.

"Put the gun against your temple."

I do. The cold metal mouth kisses my temple.

"Pull the trigger Johnny. If you won't join me then free yourself from this hell. I know you want to because you and I are alike, one and the same. This world has no place for men like us. They lock us in boxes and leave us there to rot or they pump us full of so many drugs so we can't act on the very instinct we were born with. We don't belong. We don't fit. That won't stop me, but it is stopping you, so go ahead, pull the trigger and free yourself because you don't belong in their world, and you don't belong in mine."

I don't move. The gun remains there. My finger on the trigger stays, unflinching, but there.

"Johnny. Pull the trigger."

His voice shatters inside my skull and it feels like my head will explode, but I just stare at him.

"What are you waiting for?"

I reach into that black place in my mind and from it I pull a fragment of control and with that control something follows. I aim the gun at him. My arm just points it at him. I am a passenger. However, I feel him there in my mind, fighting whatever this is.

"Drop it."

I release my gun. My right hand obeys, without question, whether I want to or not, I drop my gun, and it falls freely but it doesn't find the ground.

Hane falls back from the sudden impact, pushed back uncontrollably. His forehead explodes in a bloody web, from front and out the back, centering from a freshly opened hole. From that one small dot, his head jerks, and his skull widens from its solid state to an expanded and unnatural one. Blood rains around us and decorates me and the ground below us, outlining where we stood when he died, like a chalk silhouette. His blood. It isn't cold. It is awakening and warm and red as anyone's. I hear the loud gunshot as I catch up with consciousness. Light and blood, at least to me, move faster than sound. I look at my right hand and it is empty. I look down, on my left, and it is full. Armed with my gun, now empty, and smoking from firing its last bullet, exposed and open. Hane hits the ground, dead. I move, freely, completely on my own, for maybe the first time in a very, very long time. I drop the gun for the last time.

When Hane dies, the sound breaks through speakers, the busses PA, and the barriers speaker function normally. Loud conscious voices crack through the silence like a thunderclap, breaking the static, and it comes through loud and clear. The bus stops through smoking, screeching wheels, and comes to a full stop, just several feet from the barrier. The soldiers all lower their weapons unanimously when they hear the sentence that is being screamed at them from the busses PA.

"We are unaffected..."

My hands and body relax, and suddenly, I am the driver again. When I feel the blood course warmly through my veins, I hear a voice.

Goodbye Johnny.

Within those words that come in the form of a thought, even when I know that it is actually one part of my psyche dying off, saying goodbye to the other part that kept it alive long enough to get here. Through it, I know, finally, my fight is done forever, and with it, Greyor is gone. The bullet that failed to fire, sparing me in one moment and killing someone else in another, becomes the last bullet I will ever fire, and that bullet killed Hane. My gun bounces before settling near him and joins him, because as far as I know, this is where they both are staying. My war ends here, between the weapon I chose, and the choice I never had.

EVERY DOG HAS HIS DAY

They say that every dog knows its day. That the animal knows when it is going to die even though it doesn't tell time, it knows that it is going to die, and it seeks out the place where it will. It picks where it lays down and dies. It does this without sadness or protest. It just does. It chooses. It decides the exact moment it lets go of life and dies. I am a dog, and this is my day.

I stand above an empty six-foot deep hole that has taken me several hours to dig. This hole sits in front of a tombstone that bears my name, and up until I enter it now, has falsely marked where my body lay. I stand motionless above the gapping emptiness of the grave, with Jess' body in my arms. I step in, laying her down gently. I grab the makeshift control panel of the Bobcat utility machine; a mini dozer that holds all the dirt I dug from this grave. It hangs above the grave, ready to fill it. I have rigged the controls so I can push one button, and it'll release the dirt from wherever I am without having to sit in the driver's seat. I did this through bypassing the dead man switch.

I lay down next to Jess, with the button in my hand, and I stare up at the sky as the night fades away with the morning sun. So, this is how it ends. Every dog truly knows his day, and as the sun rises, this is mine, and my day is up. Everything they did is undone and I undid it. I was the cause and the cure. I had my war, and I ended it and won...if this is winning. At least I get to choose how and when it ends for me. I don't belong here anymore. I don't have a future, only a past. I can't live with the things I have seen or done. I can only find rest in whom I have saved and whom I have stopped. I couldn't die because I was already dead; I just needed to be buried. My finger gently rests on the button, and I exhale slowly, and as I press it, I realize in this finality after facing my enemy and seeing him, all of them die, that it is truly over and done, and so am I, after so long, and I'm relieved in the certainty that it is over. There is nothing left for me to do, except choose how I go. I look over at Jess, and whisper: "Goodbye Jellybean." And then I press the button completely and the large shovel tips and with it, dirt and darkness follows blacking out the sky, and with it I smile, and I start to speak:

"It could be worse, I could be..."

THE END